Originally from Swansea, AJ Williams has enjoyed a varied career in Visual Merchandising, Retail Management, Social Care and Education in the UK, Botswana and New Zealand. His passion for travel, world culture, the arts and history have inspired his writings.

Claire and Seren Williams

AJ Williams

THE SPIRIT OF THE STAR

AUSTIN MACAULEY PUBLISHERS™

LONDON • CAMBRIDGE • NEW YORK • SHARJAH

A CIP catalogue record for this title is available from the British Library.

ISBN 9781398444027 (Paperback)
ISBN 9781398444034 (ePub e-book)

www.austinmacauley.com

First Published 2022
Austin Macauley Publishers Ltd®
1 Canada Square
Canary Wharf
London
E14 5AA

Rita and Michael Herbert
Nicky Hall
Roni Clayden
Lynn Tisbury
Julie Franklin

Illustrations and Photographs by AJ Williams.

Table of Contents

'The World is a book, and those who do not travel read only a page.' Saint Augustine.

'You're never too old, too wacky, too wild, to pick up a book and read to a child.'
Dr Seuss.

Preface

This book is based on my travels around the world. The adventure starts when I return to the UK from New Zealand and discover a journal written by a character I have created, Bess. This had been hidden over time, now rediscovered it becomes a catalyst for my stories.

Each chapter starts with a diary extract, poem or short story from Bess' journal, which has been inspired by the countries I have visited or lived in. My daughter has inspired the second part of each chapter. I have written stories where she has her own fantasy adventures in these countries. I have created worlds based around traditional tales, Gods, mythical characters and creatures both old and new that involve magic, mystery and adventure. Therefore, whether you believe in Wonderland, Narnia, Neverland or even the Land of OZ, it is time to dream.

"If You

Dare To

Dream,

Dreams

Really

Do Come

True."   Lyrics by Yip

Harburg from Over the Rainbow.

INTRODUCTION

The Adventure Begins

Introduction

It was a day to "open up and clean the attic", Seren's mum expressed with a sigh, this being the last room in the house to be tackled. Musty smells filled the air, as Seren's mum and dad broke open a door that had been boarded up for many years. The stairs leading up to the attic were even narrower and steeper than the ones in the rest of the house. Seren hoped there would be secrets galore hidden in the forgotten, cobwebbed room at the top of the house, as she climbed in front of her parents. There was a small, circular window at one end of the room, overlooking the estuary, it let in a small amount of light, just enough to see. When it came to it the room was quite empty, a few old geography and history textbooks, a couple of oak bedroom chairs with damaged cane work and a cracked, walnut cheval mirror.

"Mum, Mum, come quick, see what I have found." Seren beckoned with such inflamed excitement.

Behind the mirror in the corner was a plain, brown, metal trunk, the type used by Victorian travellers, when going on their Grand Tour of Europe. It had a large rusty lock, broken, hanging from a frayed brown leather strap. The trunk had been well used, dented and scratched, decorated with the now washed-out painted letters E. M. Darby. Faded transport posters that had been glued to the sides of the trunk depicted pictures of South Africa, India and far-off lands once visited by its owner.

The late Georgian property where the family were living was in the parish of Whiteford near Dartmoor. The parish was so named because the church used to have a white tower, it was used by captains as a signpost to guide their ships up the Exe estuary during the shipping days. Also due to the forde that ran through the lower part of the parish. The three white cottages built in the late 1830s were situated in front of the old school. The school became the parish hall after its conversion in the 1950s, when it finally closed its doors after nearly 250 years. Next door was a blacksmith's house with the forge just a bit further up the road, now also converted to a residential property. Their cottage, the middle of the three, originally housed the school's teachers.

Seren's family moved into the cottage by early September, in time for Seren to start school. After a long journey returning from New Zealand, where they had been living. Autumn was dry and warm; summer had been extended, just for them. The cottage had been standing empty for many years, quietly waiting for somebody to come and breathe new life into its rooms. It welcomed them warmly, with open arms. The autumnal colours were vibrantly rich and deep this year whilst the soft creamy mist hung low in the valley below. Nevertheless, the crisp winter frosts arrived early in December, making the trees glisten in the silvery darkness of night. Christmas followed, the tree was dressed, the fire roared and smells of pine and cloves immersed the lounge. The family felt settled as they conjured up stories of who had lived in the house before them. While friendly ghostly images of past occupants appeared to them from time to time.

When spring came the garden bloomed with tulips and bluebells, primroses and rhododendrons. The apple tree blossomed, and then shed its petals, falling delicately like the first snows of winter. Summer arrived with its rows of scented lavender, honeysuckle and jasmine. Seren's mum and dad cleared part of the garden and found a hidden pond frequented by frogs, newts and dragonflies. Honey bees collected pollen from the wild geraniums growing around the pond. The scent of buddleia hung in the late summer air, as an army of red admirals joined the exquisite painted ladies that supped on its nectar; green woodpeckers came to visit too. The family also discovered ruined greenhouses that had been built to house an exotic plant collection. And so, the year had come and gone and the attic beckoned to be opened up.

Mum and Dad rushed over to see what Seren had discovered. She opened the trunk to discover a journal, one that had been treasured and well-kept but was forgotten over time, underneath lay a large box. Now the journal was dusty, fragmented and falling to pieces, and in need of restoration. As Seren opened it, she could see it was full of poems, paintings, sketches and daily writings by the author. There were many pressed flowers, and although their scent had gone, their colours were as vivid as the day they were pressed; all reminders of distant, romantic lands. The flowers were jacarandas and acacia berries from Africa, pōhutukawa from New Zealand. Lotus and jasmine from India, hibiscus from Fiji and a variety of other flowers such as lavender, honeysuckle, sunflowers and rhododendron, were pressed too. They were all mesmerised by Seren's find.

"What's in the box? Quick let's open it!" Seren animated in her question. They could only anticipate the prospect of what they would find.

The box contained many precious treasures that the owner must have collected on their travels. As they went through the artefacts, they imagined what an amazing life the collector must have had. First, there was a brightly coloured seed bead bracelet with a tribal pattern woven into it; it was backed with a soft leather.

"It looks like Zulu beading," Dad said. "It probably has a story or message woven into its pattern." Seren's dad had worked in Botswana and had travelled in South Africa so he had seen Zulu beading.

Then a small, delicately carved statue of a giraffe, its markings burnt into the surface of the wood.

"This is my favourite animal," said Seren. "Please can I keep it on my book case?"

"Yes, that'll be fine," Mum said. "You can imagine it running across the great Savannah."

Also, a wooden necklace with delicately, carved leopards and zebras, mingled with black and white stone beads. The next find was a porcupine quill; now was that black and white or white and black, one could never tell, but it was still very sharp! Just to one side was a delicate jewellery box decorated with soft pink and white shells. As Seren opened it the hinge squeaked, it had not been opened in many years. Inside glistened a green jade ring, a dragonfly pendant and a butterfly hair clasp.

The two insect objects almost flew out of the box with the thrill of being set free again. Both the dragonfly and butterfly wings were made of delicately transparent coloured glass that created a prism which danced in the nearby mirror. Even though they needed cleaning, their owner had adorned them. "Wow! Mum, Dad; look at their reflection in the mirror," Seren pointed.

The atmosphere in the room was now warm and magical as they all began dreaming of exotic places and lands beyond the boarded-up attic.

The next layer was Indian; a sari embedded with shisha mirrors that reflected the sunlight coming in through the round window. The sari was also delicately embroidered with soft ribbon forming elaborate flowers interwoven with coiled metallic threads. Peacock feathers fell from the sari as Seren unravelled it. There was a monkey mask and shadow puppets from Thailand. Seren wrapped the sari around her and put the mask on and holding the feathers started dancing around the attic, pretending to be a monkey. Mum and Dad laughed and started to beat the wooden floor like a drum while Seren danced in time to the rhythm.

Still more worldly treasures to be found. Next was a piece of cloth made out of soft bark fabric called tapa*. The fabric was a mottled light brown with a black print of a turtle on it used for making clothing or wall hangings. Dad said it has come from the Pacific, maybe Fiji; (having taught textiles, he would know). A small collection of illuminous blue starfish and broken bits of coral were delicately wrapped in tissue. One piece of coral was in the shape of a heart, shaped over many years, moulded by the sea. From Australia was a small didgeridoo, made of eucalyptus, painted with dreamtime scenes and animals.

Then a carving that read 'Aroha'. "That means love in Maori. I wonder if it was a gift to the owner," Mum said. Also, from New Zealand was a Maori cape woven with fragments of paua** shells and blue pukeko*** feathers. "This must have been a very special gift given in honour of someone," said Dad.

Mum then brought out two white pom poms. She said, "They were poi**** and were used in traditional Maori dancing for celebration by the girls and women." They were usually made of a material called flax, but these were a later imitation. Mum gave them a demonstration as she remembered showing the children at Play Centre when the family lived in New Zealand.

Then they found a lei from Hawaii with tulips, orchids and peonies, shades of yellow, pinks and purple that had been lovingly and delicately pressed to preserve it. "This must be very precious," Dad said, "as it contains the wearer's spirit or so tradition says. This must be looked after carefully."

Next came a pair of children's cowboy boots, well-worn, one with a damaged heel but still retained the smell of leather. A leaf pattern was intricately top stitched, with contrasting colour thread, and cut out shapes on the side of the boots. Dad said they were just like the ones his aunt and uncle sent him from America when he was young, they lived there in the late 60s.

Lastly, an item they did not recognise. A wooden stick carved with an eagle head decorated with feathers, beads and symbols of First Nation origin. Later, Seren found out it was called a talking stick. (People would pass the stick around if they had a story to tell, or something important to report.)

Just as they thought the box was empty, Seren found a faded sepia photo stuck to the side of the trunk. It was of a lady dressed in Victorian clothes standing in front of the

Statue of Liberty; on the back, it simply said 'Bess 1889'. Was this the mysterious traveller and her treasured belongings? Later Seren's dad discovered the lady in the photo was Elizabeth May Darby (known as Bess) who had lived in the house with her husband and family and that she had taught at the school. The journal was full of her travels and memories.

As time passed, the family restored the dusty old journal, which Seren took to her room and from time to time would read about Bess' adventures, and then have her own magical dreamtime experiences in far off distant lands.

*Tapa the bark of the paper mulberry tree, cloth made used in the Pacific islands.

**Poi a dance from New Zealand performed with balls attached to flax strings, swung rhythmically.

***Pāua is the Māori name given to three species of large edible sea snails.

**** The pukeko bird recognisable by its brilliant red frontal shield and deep violet breast plumage, the pukeko is interesting for having a complex social life.

SOUTH AFRICA

Chapter One, Part One:
Bess' Early Life in Devon

12th January 1849

Today I overheard ma and pa talking about joining uncle in South Africa, which is a long way away and will be a dangerous journey, with a long sea crossing.

Life has been very difficult here recently with crops failing for the farmers and not much work for my pa, who is a blacksmith. There is much poverty here.

Uncle had been the vicar of the local church here in the parish. He left several years ago to a new place in the Empire (to be Pasteur to a people who were finding God with a man called John Colenso*). There he married the daughter of a Norwegian missionary. Now he has written to pa saying we should come, as life will be better there, more opportunities with lots of families there needing blacksmiths. They have been coming from different European countries but mainly England and Holland a people he calls the Boers. What a funny name to call people I thought!

There is a company called J.C. Byrne & Co.**, uncle says, that are gathering people together and sending them to South Africa, and that pa should investigate more.

Uncle travelled with Colenso, the first bishop of Natal. He was one of the bishop's vicars, who visited mission stations. They were set up to spread the word of God to the local Zulus. Uncle wrote letters to ma and pa about his work with the Zulus, which they would read to us from time to time. The Zulus sounded very frightening, a people with a formidable history. However, they had welcomed uncle into their homes.

* Colenso was a significant figure in the history of the published word in nineteenth century South Africa. He first wrote a short but vivid account of his initial journeying in Natal, *Ten Weeks in Natal: A Journal of a First Tour of Visitation among the Colonists and Zulu Kaffirs of Natal* (Cambridge, 1855). Using the printing press he brought to his missionary station at Ekukhanyeni in Natal, and with William Ngidi he published the first Zulu Grammar and English/Zulu dictionary His 1859 journey across Zululand to visit Mpande (the then Zulu King) and meet with Cetshwayo (Mpande's son and the Zulu King at the time of the Zulu War) was recorded in his book *First Steps of the Zulu Mission*. Wikipedia.

**J.C. Byrne & Co. offered prospective emigrants a passage to Natal, during the years 1849 to 1851. Wikipedia.

The Journey to South Africa, 20th November 1849

The carriage came to a sharp holt outside the inn, jerking us awake whilst Dad snorted, causing the four black horses to chomp and chew on their bits. The pungent heat from their bodies evaporated into the chilly air as their sweat glistened making them glow.

We didn't want to leave the warmth and security of our carriage; even though it had seen better days, it was lined in cracked black leather and faded plush velvet that was still soft to feel. The driver opened the door and grunted. "Plymouth." We all alighted, causing the horses to clip their hooves in the rutted muddy lane.

The place was a bustle of people passing by, traders and merchants, sailors and gentry, even ladies in red dresses! I had never seen so many interesting looking people in one place apart from maybe on market day or harvest festival. The comforting smell of barley from the inn mixed with the waft of rotting fish. The broth, from the inns' kitchen wafted on the air and tantalised our taste buds as we waited for our bags to be unloaded.

We entered the inn where there was a roaring fire coming from the hearth. We were shown our room by the innkeeper's wife who was friendly with a ruddy complexion.

After we refreshed ourselves, we went to sit in the warm room and ate some of the broth we smelt earlier. It was then time to go to bed as we had a few busy days, making final preparations before we would board our ship to sail to Durban.

21st November 1849

The next evening, I stood overlooking the harbour with its imposing new breakwater, as the wind whipped my copper gold locks over my pale face. The autumn tides were high and were pounding at the wall below; with every white horse, my heart began to beat faster and faster. The light was becoming dimpsey but I could still see the outline of many ships in the distance. Some ships were tethered for the night whilst others still had their sails up and were being blown by the wind like the white sheets being hung out to dry on laundry day. The flickering shadowy lights from the ship's candles gave me a warm glow in the crispy coldness that tinged my cheeks. But which one was the Eclipse, the ship that was to take us to a new land, maybe it was the one I could hear with its clanking chiming bell? I wanted to cleave to what I knew but I was also excited about the future. The whipping wind around me brought with it a taste of a new and better life for my family and me.

The icy cold spray from the salty sea hit my warm lips. I licked the salt all around my teeth and inside my mouth and I began to think of what life at sea would be like for the next few months.

"Bess," as Ma liked to call me, "come away from there, it's not safe."

It brought me back to reality.

"Coming, Ma," I replied, as I started back to the Inn.

22nd November 1849

We woke to the smell of breakfast being cooked, we all got up eagerly, even my brothers, wanting to explore Plymouth Hoe, and see the Eclipse our home for the next two months. People were already up and about, fishermen preparing their rigs to go out to sea or mending their nets, sailors returning to their ships after a night out.

We watched the ships being loaded at the quay; an assortment of goods bound for the new land. There were so many shops selling wonderful things I had never seen before, trinkets brought back from around the world. There was shop selling the finest pottery, and dolls with porcelain faces. Ma and pa needed some provisions for the journey so we went to a store with a dusty wooden floor that seemed to sell everything it was like Aladdin's cave. We were allowed to buy something small so I bought a book and pencils to write and draw to keep a journal and write stories in.

25th November 1849

The ship was ready and fit for sail, it had been loaded with its cargo and food and water to last the trip. We were not the only travellers; many families were about to start a new life like us. They would become good friends over the journey and as we started our life in South Africa. Some were bound for the Cape Colony while others were bound for Natal like us.

We were all excited and started to board the ship and we were shown our space downstairs. It was very cramped and dark in the quarters below deck. We were with six other families in our section. The kitchen was small and we would all have to take turns to cook. Provisions of food were included in our passage fee.

30th November 1849

The weather was set fair as we left port and sailed out of the English Channel out to the Atlantic to hug the coast of France. However, many people were not used to the sea and took a while to find their sea legs. Excitement was set high and people's spirits were good. When we were allowed on deck we played games, while the adults would walk about and search for the coastline but mostly, they carried out duties, like cleaning, cooking, and airing our bedding.

Christmas Onboard the Ship, December 1849

Christmas was approaching and passengers and crew were getting along fine. The journey so far had been relatively mild with calm seas and we were now out in the Atlantic off the coast of Africa. On a clear day, we could see the coast, at times, what wonders and mysteries lie in the uncharted lands. My imagination got the better of me as I rested on the deck looking out into the afternoon sun.

Nevertheless, preparations needed to be made for Christmas. The captain allowed us to decorate our space below deck, ma had brought some special treats to go along with the rations we were given.

Christmas Eve had arrived and people gathered around after their supper. One gentleman had brought his ukulele which he started playing another joined in with his accordion and people started singing and dancing having fun still with a sense of excitement about the future.

Ma gathered the children around and began telling them a magical Christmas story.

From then on, the rest of the journey passed by uneventful.

Skeleton Coast (Deadly Coastline)

We had been warned of the approaching Skeleton Coast, with its deadly currents and ferocious winds that blew north and scattered ships to their doom. As we drifted quietly and eerily by, as if not to wake the dead, I stood on the deck looking towards the desolate land. Dune upon sand dune littered with shipwrecks that once carried many lost souls never to reach their destination. Surprisingly it was silent no birds in the sky no fish in the sea no wind blew. No trees or greenery on the land. I spied a lone elephant in the distance, searching for food and water. We passed by and sighed a relief.

Cape Town, 10ᵗʰ January 1850

As we approached, Cape Town the cloud hung over the bay. We had a brief lay over to collect passengers and good for Durban, our destination. A well-established port; with traders from all over the world, bartering their goods. The smells, colours. A place to return to maybe.

I asked one of the sailors, "Why is the mountain top so flat, are there always clouds above it, and why does that one look like a lion?" So, he told me a story.

How Table Mountain and Lions Head Got Their Names

"One day many years ago when time began, a giant called Tsui-goab and his friend the lion were walking in the land when they came upon the sea. They had never seen the sea before so they both sat down and wondered what to do next. The giant took out his pipe, lit it and started puffing away creating large white clouds above his head. They sat there for days trying to work out what the sea was and how they could cross it. The lion became bored and wondered off to go and get some food. He was gone for many days. When he returned, he found his friend had fallen into a deep sleep, and nothing the lion could do would wake him. The giant's pipe was still alight and was creating white clouds that floated above the giant's flat head. The lion not wanting to leave his friend again lay down next to him and also fell asleep. Over time, they were forgotten and the grass grew on top of them, the animals came to graze and then people began to settle and build homes. The locals know them as Hoerikwagga (Mountains in the Sea). They are now known today as Table Top Mountain and Lions Head."

Durban to Greytown, 20th January 1850

By the time we were awake, we had arrived at the Port of Durban. The morning sun soft and warm streamed through the small porthole. A quiet breeze rippled across the surface of the turquoise sea as the anchored ship gently rocked.

After we had breakfast and went on deck, the golden bay before us stretched as far as they eye could see. Small boats were rowing out to us to take us to shore. The ship could not get any closer due to the sand bar and current.

The small boats were loaded with luggage and passengers and the men rowed us back. An hour passed; we said our goodbyes to what had been our home for the past three months. It will be good to be on dry land again and sleep in a proper bed, but I will miss the smell and spray of the salty swaying sea.

The boats got as close to the beach as possible the tide bobbing the boats around and the women and children had to be carried off the boats to the beach. The men and boys jumped in, I wanted to jump in to but ma would not allow it. The luggage was then brought ashore.

There was much hustle and bustle; carts were brought down to transport the luggage to the dirt track, above the bay. As we got closer, we could see uncle waiting for us. It was so good to see him, after all these years, we all greeted each other.

The men loaded the luggage onto uncle's wagon. He had four large oxen to pull the wagon. It would take three days trek to get to where we were going to live in a place called Greytown. The journey was long and bumpy on the dry tracks. However, we weren't alone as there were other wagons heading our way too.

The soil was red, but not like the Devon red soil, we had left behind. When the wind picked up the loose dust was blown easily around us, so we had to cover our mouths and noses with cloth. The grass was tall, yellow, and very brittle as the sun beat down on the rocky hills.

As we kept on people would pass us walking on the road, they were very black, I had not seen many black people before. They wore no shoes and had little clothing, but had jewellery made of tiny colourful beads that jingled when they walked. They looked back inquisitively, an old lady gave me a beaming smile, so I waved back at her. During the heat of the day, we would sit or sleep inside the wagon where it was cool. At night, the wagons were moved into a circle for safety and we ate around a campfire. The bright stars filled the night sky I had never seen so many.

The next day I sat up front with uncle and he let me take the reins for a while he sat back and smiled. I felt so grown up. Then I sat and imagined many eyes watching me from the long grasses maybe a prowling lioness or cunning leopard.

After three days and two nights we finally arrived. Greytown, one dusty high street, with a few shops, a bank, a hotel, a school at one end and church at the other end. There were many folks going about their business. We passed through the street and next to the church was a pretty white house where aunt was waiting to greet us. We were all aching as we got down from the wagon. Aunt took us inside and the house smelled of fresh bread and coffee. This was their home, the vicarage.

After we were refreshed and all had our say chatting away to aunt, it was time to see our new home. The house and forge were not far from our aunt and uncle, but situated just outside the town.

The house was small but comfortable made of wood with a porch to the front and terrace to the side. The forge smelt of sulphur, iron and coal. The town had been without a blacksmith for a while and people were waiting for my dad with lots of work for him to do. So, over the next few days we settled and unpacked. Ma and I cleaned the house and reorganised the kitchen, while Dad and the boys started the forge up.

Life continued much as if we were in Devon, school, church but Dad had work and we were all happy. I helped uncle out with the small children at Sunday School. Mum would take in alterations and making clothes for the local women.

Later I would help uncle with his missionary work with the Zulus.

South Africa Missionary Work, 1854

Uncle asked me if I would like to go with him to the Missionary Station to help with the young children. He thought that I would be good at this as I help with the younger children at Sunday School. I was keen to go; ma and pa said it was OK.

I knew a little of his work, and looked forward to going. The missionary was at Umphumulo about two hours journey from Greytown. The mission was set up by Norwegian Christians whom uncle had gotten to know. There was a small hospital at the mission too.

The journey was not too difficult to make unless the rains had come, we could go and come back in a day. The ground surrounding the mission was hard and red, apart from where they grew maize. Many trees surrounded the mission, keeping the glowing white buildings cool in the hot Natal sunshine. I sometimes watched the frenzied lizards dart from tree to tree as not to burn their feet on the scorched ground.

I loved working with the young children. I would read them many stories from the bible, but as their English was little, we used to look at the pictures. We would sing songs together, play games and often make up our own stories. They would also teach me words of things in Zulu and their traditional stories. Sometimes we would go and feed the goats and chickens they kept here. I loved coming to see the children and they begged me to stay, when it was time to leave. However, they knew I would come back.

For the next three years, I would help uncle with his work during the school holidays and some weekends.

Dry Savannah

The silence of the dry savannah grass,
Is broken only by the sweet sound of the breeze,
Being carried across on open plains,
It whispers as it bends the reeds delicately,

One way then the next.

As I sit on a rocky outcrop (kopjies) above the watering
hole,
At the place where the sun rises,
Where leopards once dared to roam,
Guinea fowl scratch by and a hoopoe uncurls his crown,
Two warthogs bathe snortly in the mud, twitching tails, when
flies dare to pass by.
Large red termite mounds dot the landscape,
The intricate tunnelled lives of their inhabitants,
Only disturbed by shifting sands,
And long worm-tongued anteaters,
Tall and pinnacle, life in an underground-overground,
African fortress.

Armoured bush crickets scratch their back legs,
Constant chirping, chirping echoes across the Veldt,
As the golden sun begins to reach its peak,
the noise intensifies to deafening levels
As shimmering images cast a spell on horizon's plateau,
The peace only to return in the beating midday heat.

The afternoon brings delicate, melodic tones of the Zulu
choir,
Umbrellaed by a red-berried acacia tree,
The children are joined by the female voices then the deep
rich male tones,
Individual voices break out as some clap while others stamp
their feet,

The sound of bells and beads echo in harmony sending chills
down my spine.

Wood-gathering, head-stick carrying women pass by,
For evening supper to prepare of delicious mouth-watering
lamb stew,
With decorated earthen pots on smokey, spitting open fires
Families start gathering to feast and tell the tales of the day
Time for me to go and enjoy my own family.

As evening breeze cools and dusky light approaches,
Lightning bugs arrive to twilight the violet sky,
They flitter by as elegant as Cleopatra* on delicate wings,
Mesmerising here and there, now and again,
As golden fairies that dare to linger far too long.

At the setting sun, drums beat slowly to its descending,
The skyline slowly disappears to a burning empyrean**,
The fire crackles and glows, attracting large African moths,
Illuminous to velvety touch, uncurling wings they glide to
the light of the moon,
As ancient ancestral spirits dance in the last flickering
embers of the fire.

*A type of firefly.
** The highest heaven, supposed by the ancients to
contain the pure element of fire.

Chapter One, Part Two:
The Day Seren
Became a Leopard

Saturday afternoon, lounging on the sofa, Seren's dad was watching Zulu, again! A film that he had seen in the cinema as a child, one that had captured his imagination about the Zulus and South Africa. Little did he know that years later he and Seren's mum would trek to Rourke's Drift and Islawanda to visit the actual places. Seren by now was feeling bored and went to read the journal she had found. Sitting on her bed, looking at the pictures that Bess had painted of the many animals that can be seen in South Africa; the most impressive of all was the painting of a leopard.

Through the wall Seren could hear the Zulus beating their shields and their deep voices resonating their battle song, it sounded like there was a storm brewing. Her heart racing to the vibration of the skinned shields being struck by the warrior's Iklwa. Her hands became clammy as the sound of an African storm rumbled around in the distance. The purple-grey sky was lit up with flashes of silver, the rain pelting down as it bounced off the scorched red soil, was it Devon soil or an African landscape? A dreamy gunmetal fog surrounded Seren, as a violent storm approached from the charcoal skyline. When the fog cleared, she realised the air was much warmer and a heavy, damp, earthy smell hung all around.

Families were sheltering in their thatched roundels, out of the clicking rain, hitting and bouncing off the hard-broken dry ground. A young Zulu girl, called Nokwazi, came over, held Seren's hand, and beckoned to her to come in out of the rain. Seren followed.

Nokwazi, (which means daughter of wisdom). Her mum named her this for on the day that she was dedicated, she lifted her up to the Sky Gods and they blessed her with wisdom.

It was smoky inside Nokwazi's home, but comforting. There was a pot of sweet-smelling stew cooking over the fire. The mother asked if she would like some and Seren smiled and said, "Yes, please." Nokwazi's mum, dad, and older sister then sat down around the fire, to eat the stew. They were then joined by their grandma and Nokwazi's uncle and brother.

After they had all eaten, the rain had stopped. Nokwazi's brother went with his dad to check the cattle were OK. Her mum collected the dishes to wash up and told the older daughter to go and get fresh water from the stream. Nokwazi was free to play, they left saying goodbye to grandma who was singing to herself. Seren and Nokwazi went to look at the animals that her family kept. They had lots of goats in a fenced area enclosed by thorn bush branches; where chickens were scratching around for small bugs in the red soil. The goats were of different shades of brown and some were mixed with patches of black and white, they were very inquisitive when the girls went to the gate. They bleated loudly and the girls patted their course hair.

The family kept cattle in a kraal far from the village; but closer by they had a mother and calf. The mother was not well and the calf was failing to feed properly, and so they were able look after them both. Nokwazi was able to get some milk, from her mum, and they were able to feed the calf. He came running over to them happy to see if they had some food for him. He latched onto the long narrow pot, covered in cow hide and supped away, milk dribbling from the side of his mouth. The milk was soon gone, but he stayed with them for a while, so the girls could smooth him.

"He's called Omncane, Little One," said Nokwazi. "Do you have any animals at home?" she asked Seren.

"I have a tabby cat called Boots," replied Seren "she is called that because she has long white legs that look like she has boots on. She came from a rescue centre. One day I would like to have a dog and I like pigs very much; they are so cute."

The girls then went for a walk close to the river where it was safe. Nokwazi asked Seren what her favourite wild cat was. Seren said it was a leopard, because of their ability to survive, and the way they would drape themselves over tree branches and overlook the savannah. Nokwazi said she was very frightened of leopards, as sometimes they would come and take their goats and then they would then go hungry.

Nearby was a rocky outcrop with large flat boulders where they went to play. Seren said, "Let's pretend to be leopards." Seren with her red hair became the most magnificent leopard, with a very unusual strawberry coloured coat, whilst Nokwazi pretended to be one of her cubs. They spent the afternoon lounging on the rocks and dozing as it was very hot. When the day's heat started to dissipate, they decided it was time to go hunting. They moved very slowly from the warm grey boulders onto the plain, which they had been surveying. The grass was long and cooling, it provided a good covering so they could not be seen by their prey. First of all, they went to drink at the watering hole. The elephants were already there so they had to be careful, elephants can be very tetchy and they did not want to upset them. So, they went down wind of them to drink. The water was so refreshing.

They went to sit in the grass and see what took their fancy. When the elephants finally left, the buffalo and giraffe came to drink. Then it was the turn of the zebra and wildebeest. Lastly came the antelopes just as it was becoming dusk. The herd of impala looked particularly tasty, but they were very fast. The pair started to slink closer and closer to the impala not wanting to be seen or to scare them. Several days had passed since they had last eaten. Sitting still in the grass waiting patiently, finally one of the impalas broke away from the main group. Seren told Nokwazi to stay put whilst she went even closer. The impala lifted its head twitching its nose, something was on the air, and it went back to munching on the sweet grass. Then Seren saw her chance, she leapt and pounced from the grass, the impala realised the trouble she was in and started to make a dash for it. Seren followed swiftly, dashing this way and that, following the impala and getting ever closer, her taste buds scenting the air and saliva dribbling from her mouth. Almost there, almost, her claws ready to pounce; then something happened that Seren was not expecting. She picked up a different scent one she didn't like, lion. She abandoned the chase changing direction and headed back to Nokwazi. Good! She was safe. The lions were returning to the area, this was not good news for Seren and Nokwazi. They headed to the safety of the rocks for the night, hungry, but safe. Throughout the night the lion's roars echoed and boomed, defiantly, kings of the savannah.

The next day saw the sunrise as usual and time for the strawberry leopard and her cub to find a new safe home away from the lions. They wandered for days and eventually found a safe place with lots of cover, fresh water and more importantly food. The next day the leopard made a kill and they feasted on fresh impala. But they would have to move on from time to time, when the lions came a calling.

The two girls finished their adventure and returned to Nokwazi's family. The storm was still rumbling around in the distance and there were sharp golden and silver streaks of lightening in the sky.

Inside the communal homestead there were lots of activities going on. Some of Nokwazi's friends were making bead necklaces and bracelets, with lots of different patterns and colours. Others were dancing and the smaller children were sat in a circle playing a game with small stones that were being thrown into a pottery bowl. The women were busy at their chores, the older women were sat chatting and the men were off hunting while the boys were pretending to be hunters.

"Would you like to make something?" Nokwazi asked Seren.

"I would but you will have to show me."

They sat down and Nokwazi got a small loom that had two short wooden sticks either side with string holding them together, it was in fact made from cow sinews. The needle was made from filed goat bones. Nokwazi showed Seren how to pick up the beads with the needle and attach them between the sinews on the loom, there were four beads to a strand, she would then pass the needle back through the four beads to secure them. She continued for a little while picking up the beads and altering the colour to change the pattern. The colours were of blue for happiness, yellow for wealth and white for love. Then once Seren had got the hang it she continued weaving the beads back and forth until she got to the end. Then Nokwazi trimmed the ends of the loom and secured them with larger beads and a wooden hook so Seren could attach it to her wrist.

While Seren was making her bracelet, Nokwazi's older sister and her friends were practicing a dance. Seren asked Nokwazi was it a special dance to which she replied, "It was called the Reed Dance, performed by girls when they were ready to become a woman. It was a very special dance and only performed once a year, over several days in September, springtime in Zululand." Nokwazi said. "The dance is a celebration of their culture and the girls get to dress up in beautiful brightly coloured and beaded costumes. It's very exciting as they get to meet the Zulu princess who leads all the girls in a particular dance where they make a sea of colour and present a gift of reeds laying them at the king's feet and this is in honour of the original ancestor who emerged from a bed of reeds."

Nokwazi pulled Seren up by the hand and started showing her some of the steps she had learnt from her grandma. They started to imitate the older girls, who were taking the dance practice very seriously, Seren and Nokwazi started giggling and laughing. Grandma told them to be quiet so they sat back down to continue their beading. Embarrassed Nokwazi covered her smile with her hand.

After Seren had been taught how to do the beading and a few of the dance steps the girls went outside to sit. By now, it had got dark and the stars started coming out one by one to light up the Ebusuku Isibhakabhaka.

"This is the dwelling place of all the divine beings like Unkulunkulu 'The Greatest One' and Nokhubulwane the 'Goddess of Rain' and where the spirit of the dead live." Nokwazi told Seren.

Seren asked Nokwazi what star was in Zulu to which she replied "Inkanyezi."

"So, my name in Zulu is Moya Inkanyezi, which means the 'Spirit of the Star'," said Seren (Seren is Welsh for star). Nokwazi nodded to agree.

"Do all the stars have names?" asked Seren.

As they looked into the velvet sky Nokwazi pointed them out. "That one is called Dithutlwa the Giraffes but sometimes called Lion Paws. The bright one is called InKhwenkwezi the Brilliant star and that one is called the Female Steenbok, the one that looks like a scorpion is called the Fire Finishing star."

The stars looked very different from the sky Seren was used to seeing. "Is there one called the leopard star?" asked Seren.

"There are a group of red stars, very faint, just above the horizon," Nokwazi pointed in their direction.

Seren could see a faint cluster of reddish stars that patterned like a leopard with two brighter stars above that looked like eyes. Seren asked how it got its name.

Grandma came over to tell Nokwazi it was time to sleep.

"Grandma, can you tell us a story about how the leopard star got its name?"

"Cosu," Nokwazi asked her grandma to speak "little by little," so Seren would understand.

"Kwesukasukela," the grandma started to tell a story.

The Hunters in the Night Sky

"Long ago there were a group of umzingeli searching for food on the Great Plains, when they came across an old woman, Isalukazi*. The old woman was trying to draw water from a kahle amanzi, she asked if they might help her. But they refused to. So, the old woman cursed them and said that they would never see another day apart from looking down from above. They just laughed at her and moved on. But that night as they fell asleep under the stars, a great storm blew up covering them in the red soil and sent them up to the sky. As they were in a cluster like hunters, they became known as the Red Leopard at night because of the pattern they formed."

Seren became sleepy, listening to grandma, as smoke started to drift into the sky from the fire. As she looked to the stars they seemed to move in the haze.

Seren could see the umzingeli moving across the horizon in a pack, and then they spread out. The other starry animals such as the giraffe and steenbok got twitchy. The hunters threw their umkhonto through the sky which looked like inkanyezi entwizayo flying through the atmosphere and burning up the blackness. Then the lion star appeared to move, placing his paws over the bright moon to dim its glowing light, enabling him to hunt better. The hunters knew they could not compete with the lion so they returned to the safety of the horizon. As the earth turned, the hunters drew back together and slipped silently below the horizon. There was a shriek from above as the lion's paws retreated from the moon. The moon now bright again, settled high in the indigo darkness its glory outdoing the stars, which faded into the background.

"Cosu, cosu yaphela," said the grandmother.

"Siyabonga, ibimnandi," replied Seren.

The girls had a wonderful time but now it was time for Seren to say hamba kahle to Nokwazi and her family. The hugged and waved goodbye to each other. Nokwazi invited Seren to come back at any time.

Seren rubbed her eyes, sat up, and realised she was back in her bedroom. She peered through her bedroom window, by now it was dark. She looked at the stars to see if she recognised any from her dream. But they formed different constellations. She thought of Nokwazi and wondered if she was doing the same.

Seren returned to the lounge, where her dad was still watching Zulu! She showed him the painting of the leopard from Bess' journal and told him of the adventurous dream she had. He was fascinated by her tale and loved the painting, which they later hung on the wall.

*Isalukazi: Who can also be seen in the stars and is known as the constellation the 'Old Bag of the Night'.

Glossary

Iklwa: Short stabbing spear.

Ebusuku Isibhakabhaka: The African night sky.

Cosu Cosu: Little by little.

Kwesukasukela: Once upon a time.

Umzingeli: Hunters.

Kahle Amanzi: Well.

Umkhonto: Spears.

Inkanyezi Entwizayo: Shooting stars.

Cosu, cosu yaphela: And so, bit by bit it is finished.

Siyabonga, ibimnandi: Thank you that was very interesting.

Hamba kahle: Goodbye.

BOTSWANA

Chapter Two, Part One:
Land of the Upside-Down Tree

Bechuanaland (Now Botswana) – A Protectorate of the British Empire, September 1857

Pa says Annie and I must travel north with uncle to visit Bechuanaland. Partly to keep him company on his quest to meet the King and Queen, they recently converted to Christianity and he says they need help and have requested a missionary. Uncle is the closest minister to them so it must be him that goes. The bishop of Durban wants him to go, as uncle works so well with the Zulus.

Also, there is talk of lung disease coming up from the south, father says I must stay away and not get ill. Jacob had it when he was younger and survived, he was strong. The youngsters are too young to travel. I am 16, Annie is now 12 and the younger ones, Thomas is 7 and Benjamin is 5. It was decided in the end, that Annie would stay with our uncle's wife while we were away. To keep her company and to help with their young children.

Uncle was kind to me so I was looking forward to the journey. We waited till spring to make the journey more bearable, from the cold nights of winter, and we would return the following autumn.

The journey started with a four-day and three-night trek to Johannesburg. We packed uncles' wagon full with supplies.

We passed the imposing Drakensburg, snow still sitting on the highest peaks. A chilly breeze flowing from the mountain tops kept us moving at a steady pace. The rocky red land was little inhabited from the Drakensburg to our first destination, apart from outlying hardened Boer settlements and farmers. All struggling to make a living, especially the cattle farmers who would have the occasional infringement with rustling Zulus.

Spring grass and flowers started sprouting and ice melt water begun to fill the streams.

We arrived in Johannesburg a very different place from Greytown. This being a Boer stronghold. I was glad to move on I do not find the Boers to my liking. After a few nights resting in Johannesburg, it was time to carry on the journey.

We reached the dry Limpopo River the border between South Africa and Beuanchland. We followed the riverbed for a few days with its yellow grass and shrubs before turning North West. Occasionally people would appear from the bush to greet us and stare at us. They looked different from the Zulus in appearance and clothing. They were smaller had rounder faces and paler skin. Their clothing was simpler just animal skin and plain beading. Occasionally we would get glimpses of small troops of baboons and small antelope, apart from that the land seemed pretty barren.

We would camp out under the starry night; wisps of smoke would rise up into the cloudless sky. Uncle would make up stories for me, until I fell asleep. I would them dream until he woke me with the smell of coffee brewing and bacon sizzling over the fire, he had restarted from the embers of the night before.

It took a whole week to travel to King Sekgoma's residence at Shoshong, he was chief of the Bamangwato tribe. They had been expecting us and their warmth was welcoming. The girls and boys danced us into the Kings compound where he and his Queen greeted us with big smiles. Two women came forward and placed woven beaded bands upon our heads. The dancers continued, as their feet slapped the ground, the dried seed husks around their ankles jingled. The rhythm of the dance was infectious and full of happiness.

After we had rested and washed, we were treated to a delicious goat stew followed by more singing and dancing. We slept well in our straw beds that night.

Over time, while we were in the village uncle spent many hours talking to the King about God, while I spent time with the Queen and her children, playing under the jacaranda trees. I would also read them stories as they fell asleep in the heat of the afternoon. Sometimes I would help the women prepare the seswaa and pap for the evening meal.

Uncle would call church on a Sunday and more and more people came from the outlying area, at the King's request. They loved their singing, our hymns and their songs begun to merge into inspirational, mesmerising sounds.

Once a week the village folk would also meet at the Kgotla (public meeting place). Where they would spend hours discussing things that affected the village. They loved to debate but everybody was listened to that wanted to speak and then they would vote and the King would make a decision based on what had been said.

The King was so pleased with uncle that he invited us to stay with him at his summer residence, miles to the north of the country. He said it was the most special place in the world, he called it the Okavango. It had oasis of trees surrounded by lagoons of covered lilies and floating sweet tasting water chestnuts. It was a haven for many beautiful birds, wild animals and a great place to fish. Moreover, in this dry and dusty land it sounded like heaven.

We travelled with the King's party through Serowe, onto the Makgadikgadi Salt Pans. We camped one night at the pans where we unsettled a big flock of flamingos. Layer upon layer of pink rose elegantly from the snow-white encrusted saltpans. The flamingos merged with the golden violet sunset as they flew off towards the horizon.

The next day we set off from Maun. From there we took to the reeded river on mokors winding our way to a large island on the delta where the King had his summer home.

After a lovely time there, it was time to return to Shoshong and for uncle to finish his work. A month after arriving back a new missionary had arrived and with him, he brought a letter from ma saying that all was well at home and it was safe for me to return. It was sad to leave all our new friends but it was time to go home.

Land of the Upside-Down Tree

Thunderous purple and silvery rain are released over distant skies with dramatic electrifying effects.

After a long wait the rain finally floods the delta, waterways burst and lakes are filled afresh,

To quench this scorched, dry and dusty earth, the land of the Upside-Down Tree.

Red lechwe powerfully and gracefully leap from oasis to oasis, as hoopoe birds dance a strange dance as life slowly returns.

The sun glistens and sparkles over water that has travelled miles to reach its final destination.

Our adventure begins in the land of the Baobab Tree.

Mokoros float and drift lazily through a maze of papyrus reeds and bulrushes.

As we watch green and yellow weaver birds suspend their spherical new homes from palm trees.

We enter lagoons of endless lilies; the hum of dragonflies which fill the stillness as they hover in the scented air.

Water chestnuts float sweet as candy and quench our thirst in the intense heat.

We take tea where a Hippo lie to sleep and listen to their distant deep bellows ripple and vibrate beneath the waters' surface.

As we shelter under a cooling canopy in the midday sun, the lilac breasted rollers twitter and keep us company.

Elephants reach for fermenting amarulas on high, their trunks swaying to the beat of slow drums.

A monitor lizard slinks beneath his tree as his tongue sniffs the air for, he is awoken by monkeys chattering above.

Fish eagles soar high on warm African currents as kingfishers dive for small prey.

Catfish break the waters' surface to feed on insects above, while sacred ibis stalk the riverbank edge, as we slowly slither by.

Blue wildebeest come out from the shade to graze on lush savannah grass and drink from sweet waters.

The day's heat begins to subside and the fiery sun starts to glow amber and orange over the deep violet horizon, now it is time to return to camp.

At night, we sit and listen to the chirp of insects galore, fire flies buzz and glow in the moonlit camp as moths float to their demise in the lamp's flame.

The heady musk of the red soil lays heavy on the air, carried by the warmth of the evening breeze, deep into our nostrils.

Blackness is alight with colourful stars that fill the vast African night sky, as we reflect on our day snaking through the labyrinth of islands and grasses.

Morning beckons as we are woken by cheeky monkeys swinging from tree to tree, the smell of the fresh morning dew and the vibrant bright light.

The reed covered path carries us from our stilted hut, across buffalo grass and mangroves; as the waters reach their final destination they rise up and evaporate into the land beyond the Baobab Tree.

Our journey south will take us back through salt pans and termite nesting grounds, where flamingo, ostrich, giraffe and secretary birds roam freely, oh for the land of the Upside-Down Tree.

Chapter Two, Part Two: Tales from Botswana

Seren was on holiday in Turkey, with her family, in a place called Dalyan; they had decided to take a boat trip down the river to the beach. Along the way, tall grasses edged the riverbank. Herons and egrets were flying high and landing ever hopeful of catching an unsuspecting fish. As the boat travelled further down the river, twisting around many bends the river became a network of channels. Seren's dad said it reminded him of the time they were in the Okanvango Delta in Botswana, being guided on a mokoro*.

Seren imagined what it would be like there and remembered that Bess had travelled to the Okanvango (when she had visited Bechuanaland now Botswana with her uncle). The water was gently lapping at the sides of the boat; Seren let her fingers ripple its cool surface, the sun high overhead a fish eagle screeched, circling on a warm current of air. Drifting slowly into a hazily sleep the river started to change, then Seren caught something out of the corner of her eye. It moved very fast and with a huge splash disappeared into the river. Surely, it couldn't be a crocodile, could it? The scenery had changed from the river inlet in Turkey to the slow-moving riverbanks of the Okavango Delta.

The boat pulled up alongside a small jetty. As Seren looked up, she could see a fish eagle high in the sky and a boy standing on the jetty who helped her off the boat. "Welcome to my village," he said, "I hope you have had a good journey; I have been waiting for you. You must be tired?" the boy asked.

Seren said she was fine but hungry.

"Oh good," said the boy, "Mma has just made a large pot of sesswa** and pap."

As they sat around and enjoyed the food the boy asked, what Seren would like to do? She said she would like to see a giraffe her favourite animal and a baobab tree, as she remembered seeing a painting that Bess had done of one and Seren thought it could not be a real tree.

The boy Kagiso, whose name means Peace, told Seren a legend about how the baobab tree got its name.

"We call the tree 'the upside-down tree.' When bare of its leaves, the spreading branches of the Baobab look like roots sticking up into the air as if it had been planted upside-down.

An African legend tells that the baobab was amongst the first trees to appear on Earth. When the palm tree, the flame tree and the fig tree appeared, the Baobab began to grumble that it wanted to be taller, to have brilliant flame-coloured flowers, and bear tasty fruit too. The Gods grew angry at this incessant wailing and pulled up the tree by its roots, and replanted in upside down to keep it quiet!" ***

"Let's go for a walk," suggested Kagiso, "down to the lake. We have three orphaned, baby elephants that come to visit us; they will walk with us too!"

Seren was very excited, as she had never seen elephants so close.

"We have to feed them, when they visit; we have also given them their names," said Kagiso.

As they approached, they raised their trunks to sniff the air, they tickled Seren as they sniffed her hair. Kagiso introduced each one in turn to Seren; Thandi, Seena and Sukuri. The five of them walked to the lake through the bush, the elephants one in front of the other with the two children leading them. The sand was very slippery beneath their feet, Kagiso wore no shoes but his feet were used to the hot sand and the sharp thorns buried in the ground.

Jacaranda trees and bright red fire lilies lined the track; their scent infused the air. The elephants would stop from time to time reaching their trunks up to the sweet fresh leaves at the top of the acacia trees.

As they walked further on, they came across the enormous baobab tree, Kagiso said this was the oldest one here and they thought it was about 3000 years old. Seren was speechless as she thought it was magnificent. They spent time playing around the tree.

It was time to move on to the lake. As they approached the lake the elephants started to get very excited swinging their trunks at the thought of the deep sweet water where they could cool off. They got to the edge of the lake and Seren could see two tiny ears and eyes staring at them from the middle of the lake.

"Hippopotamuses," said Kagiso, "we must stay back!" Another set of ears and eyes appeared and started moving closer and closer to the bank. The elephants wanted to move into the water but were nervous of the approaching hippos. The hippos came up to the edge of the water but would not come out of their safety space. They sized each other up. Then the hippos snorted water and off they swam. The elephants had won the battle and moved into the lake to cool off, spraying water over themselves.

Seren and Kagiso sat in the shade of an acacia tree eating a sweet ground melon to quench their thirst. The elephants would occasionally spray them both with a little water as they thought they needed cooling down!

Then in the distance on the other side of the lake appeared a family of giraffes that had come down to drink. Seren watched in wonder at their statuesque elegance. They had to do the splits in order to lower their long neck to drink. It was very strange; Seren hoped they would not get stuck. There was a baby giraffe; Seren thought that it was very cute. She wanted to go and pat it, but she knew it would not be safe.

As they sat there, Kagiso told Seren tales of Botswana.

*a traditional carved out canoe.

**Pounded beef or goat meat.

*** http://ezinearticles.com/?Baobab-Tree---Interesting-Facts-and-Fiction&id=4214639

How Giraffe Got His Long Neck and Legs

One day long ago when the desert was lush and green, there lived many animals but they all looked very much the same, just different colours. They would gather around the water hole at sunset and discuss many different things. Elephant, Giraffe, Rhino, Hippo and Zebra were all there. In those days Elephant had small ears, Giraffe had a short neck, Rhino had no horns, Hippo was much like he is today just a bit smaller and Zebra was either black or white but not both.

One evening, one of the animals suggested that it would be good if they all looked a little different, so the people could tell them apart. They all agreed and had a long discussion, for they liked to discuss everything at length and in great detail about how it could happen. Well, this is a tale about Giraffe, so we will see how he got his long neck and legs.

One afternoon Elephant and Giraffe were walking in the savannah when Giraffe looked up and saw many delicious green leaves at the top of the tree.

He said to Elephant, "It's a shame about those green leaves at the top of the tree, as nobody can reach them and they always go to waste." However, Elephant used his long trunk, grabbed the top of the tree, and brought down the sweetest tasting leaves Giraffe had ever tasted for him to munch on. They were delicious Giraffe thought I could get used to them.

That night Giraffe went home, dreamt of the sweet leaves, in his dream his neck had grown long so that he could get the leaves for himself, how elegant he thought he looked too. In the morning when he woke, he still had a short neck though. All day he planned how he could make his neck long, but he failed to come up with a solution.

The next day he thought he would go and visit the wise old Baboon that lived in the great tree on the plains. It was a long walk but he got there by evening. It was chilly on the plains and the stars were shining brightly that night. He called for the wise Baboon who came down from his tree and listened to Giraffe's story.

He sat for a while then jumped up and went back up his tree chanting. Giraffe waited and waited, the moon came up and smiled at him and started to shine across the night sky. By the time Baboon came back, singing, the moon had sunk below the horizon and the morning sun had started to rise creating a mystical shade of indigo.

"Well," said Giraffe.

"Ah be patient my son, this will take time," the wise Baboon replied.

"You must come back in three days' time when the moon is at its fullest. Between now and then you must bathe in the muddy pool near the flat black rocks every day for two hours, you may smell pretty bad but it will be worth it."

Giraffe did as he was asked and went back three days later when the moon was full.

"I am back, wise old Baboon," he called to him.

He waited a while the then Baboon came down chattering away to himself. Giraffe could see he was carrying something.

"Good, now you must drink this special potion I have prepared for you, drink it all mind you. Then you will grow long legs and a long neck, and be able to enjoy the sweet leaves. But there may be some side effects; I don't know what good or bad. You smell a bit too," he said.

Giraffe drank the sweet sticky potion and licked his lips. He then went to sleep. He dreamt that his legs grew long and that his neck stretched to reach the green leaves. However, as he grew, the mud that had set on him began to crack, and as he used his new long tail to swish it away, he was left with the most beautiful markings. He said to himself how beautiful and elegant I am.

When he woke to his surprise this time, he really had grown. He couldn't wait to show his friends. When all the other animals saw Giraffe and how wonderful and amazing, he looked, they wondered that if the wise old Baboon could make them look different and unique.

How Cheetah Got Her Spots

One day while the sun beat down on the scorched land, the animals came as usual to the waterhole. Even here, the water was drying up, the rains were late, and the animals were getting very thirsty and worried, as the flood should have arrived by now. So, they decided to send out groups in search of water.

The elephants went in one direction, the giraffes in another, the zebras and wildebeests went together. The wild cats, the stocky lions, the slim Cheetah and the agile Leopard all followed. (At this point, all the cats looked similar; they were the same colour and only looked different in their size and shape).

The only animal to remain behind was Hippo, as he needed to stay in the little water left to stop his skin from burning.

The lions followed the animals for food, they would hunt in packs so they were successful at catching their pray.

However, as Cheetah and Leopard hunted alone it was more difficult for them.

Leopard and Cheetah got together one day and decided they needed to be different from the lion to catch their prey. They needed to blend in with the background more so they could get closer to their prey by sneaking up on them, keeping the surprise for longer. They wondered how they could make this happen. They thought and slept on it.

The next day Cheetah said, "What if we stuck leaves on us to make us look like the trees."

It seemed like a good idea, but all the leaves fell off with the first gust of wind.

"How about trying feathers," suggested Leopard. They tried this idea but they scratched too much. "Glad we are not birds," said Leopard.

Next, they tried snakeskin to blend in, but this they found too smelly and the animals they were stalking got the scent of snake and ran away. They did not know what else to do. They sat in shade beneath the great trees at the edge of the savannah. As they dozed in the afternoon heat, the monkeys in the trees began chattering and woke Leopard out of his daze. The sun was high and shining through the trees, and as Leopard lazily looked, he could see the reflection of the leaves creating a shimmering pattern on ground, causing Cheetah to blend into the background.

"Where are you?" Leopard called out searching for Cheetah.

"I am here," replied Cheetah. Then as she moved Leopard could see her again.

"That's it," he said, "the pattern created from the reflection of the leaves has made you invisible. If we can get the pattern to stay, we can hunt more successfully."

"We must go to the wise Baboon to see if he can help us create these patterns permanently on us," said cheetah. So off they went to find him.

When they found him, he was walking up and down chanting to himself as usual. So, they sat and waited for him to stop, then he realised he was being watched.

"Humm, what do you two want?" he asked.

They explained their situation to him and he agreed to help them. He gave them a special ooze clay that they needed to rub into their fur that would protect it from the sun. But in return there was a price to pay, to look different from the lions. That was that Cheetah and Leopard would never live, in family groups like the lions but would always live alone, to wonder the grasslands, and live, in fear of the lions. A price they were prepared to live with.

So, they rubbed and rubbed the clay on parts of their body and went back to sit under the trees. They both chose different trees with different leaf shapes. Then leaving the sun, the leaves and the clay to do their work, they dozed. After the sun had gone down, they licked the clay off each other, to be left with special markings all over their body. They were very pleased with the results and put it to the test straight away. So off they went to hunt.

After that, the rains came and the delta was flooded once more. The animals returned to the waterhole, where Hippo was still bathing in the mud, wondering when his friend would return. As they did, he let out a large yawn to welcome them back saying how much he had missed them all.

With that Kagiso finished his stories.

The sun was setting and it was time to walk back home with the elephants and give them some milk. After Seren helped to feed them, it was time for her to go. She hugged Kagiso and said thank you to him for such a wonderful day. He helped back onto the boat and he waved her goodbye.

Back on the Dalyan River, Seren woke from her sleep, mesmerised by the sound of the boat chugging up the river. The large bird Seren had seen earlier had caught his evening fish supper and was now feeding on the river bank.

The captain asked if she would like to have a go at navigating the boat home which she did with relish. The boat returned to the harbour, where it moored. Everyone was tired after a long day at the beach, as they got off the boat, Seren sighed. "What an adventure we had."

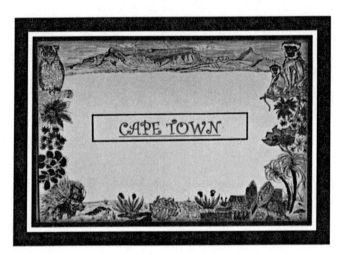

CAPE TOWN

Chapter Three, Part One:
Cape Town, 1861 to 1872

At the age of twenty, I got the opportunity to move to Cape Town to be a governess through a contact my uncle had with the church in Cape Town. I sailed from Durban to Cape Town. The journey took ten days on the coastal steamer the Waldensian. The family met me at the dock. Mr and Mrs Brockenhurst with their three children, May, Charles and Henry. I could see my work was cut out but I was up for the challenge. The family had recently arrived from England and were unable to bring their governess with them. They lived in a grand town house in the newly created artist area of Cape Town. The avenue was lined with bougainvillea and jacaranda trees, at this time of year they were in full bloom, adding to the creative ambiance. The house had a clear inspiring view of Table Mountain.

Days turned into weeks and week into months, I missed my family and wrote to them often but the Brockenhursts were very kind to me. After church on Sundays, (these precious afternoons were my only free time after a busy week with the children), if it was a pleasant day, I would spend the time at the Kirstenbosch Botanical Gardens with their colourful display of flowers and plants, sometimes taking time to painting them. With my newly made friends we would go to the gardens together.

One day my friends and I noticed a new young gardener. He would smile at me on occasion and I found out that his name was Theo. One day I plucked up enough courage to speak to him. After that, we would walk through the gardens and he would tell me the Latin names of the flowers. We never saw him at church, but I introduced him to the Brockenhursts, and they knew of his family back in England. We started courting and fell in love. In 1869, we were married and Theo told me of his plans for the future.

As part of our honeymoon, we were able to go back to visit my parents. While we were there travelling, we saw the new sugar plantations growing. There was indigenous sugar cane in the area, but it was not sweet enough to export. Theo met a contact who wanted him to travel to India to help with the plantations there. With Theo's experience, it would be a great opportunity. We decided to look into the possibility more; Theo would travel to India on his own to check out the situation. While Theo was travelling back and fore to India, I fell pregnant and Charles was born in 1870. On his last return from India, Theo was very excited and so the decision was made to leave for India in 1872. It was time to say goodbye to our home in Africa never to return. India possessed a new adventure for us.

The day arrived for us to leave and we would sail from the Alfred Basin in Table Bay on the Windsor Castle (its maiden voyage) from London en-route to Calcutta. The mist lay low over the mountain today as if it was sad to see us go. The Brockenhursts were there to wave us off to our new land and the promise that India had to offer. The family had been so good to me over the past years, it brought tears of sadness to say goodbye. However, part we must as our worldly belongings, which did not amount to much, were being loaded into the ships hold. A low hum rung out over the harbour from a church choir singing in the distance. It was quiet and soothing as was the sea. The anchor raised and we left the quayside. A chill came over me as my heart jumped a beat and my stomach churned yearning for what I was to leave behind, my life, my home, friends and family, everything I knew. Nevertheless, I had done it before, even though they were not my decisions. This time it was my choice to start a new life in a new land. As we left the safety of Table Bay, my heart told me this would not be the last time; I would do this.

Cape Town by Bess

<u>Te amo dilectus meus in aeternum</u>
My time amongst the Protea of Cape Town
The city of vibrant markets and gumboot dancers.
Where clouds settle on the flat mountain top,
That rises beyond the vast veldt, plateaued with fragrant
colourful flowers.
As settlers crossed the great Karoo on wagon trains to
hardship and adventure,
For the Limpopo lined their way to the land of the Zulus.
The clouds waterfall off the hillside to the natural harbour
below,
Where the sounds of soft African voices rise up to meet their
white aurora.
While still, the hues of Dutch spices linger from markets
stalls and ships of old,
To the distant golden bays and rippling waves,
Where the sands of time shed a tear for such beauty lies
beyond.
While the spirit of life dwells within,
The Lion at its heart roars for freedom and equality.
Travellers passed by the Cape of Good Hope,
Only to rest their souls on a deadly skeleton coast.
'Beyond lay vineyards, sun bleached with
winter sunshine frost and mist,
They produce a nectar that is blessed by the Gods.
Whilst my time of, walking and freedom,
Amongst the botanical gardens knows no constraints or fear
of time.

My heart is not lost for I spy love from a distance.

He creates, digs and plants to his heart desire.

Doth, he know I even exist?

I stop, sketch and paint the beauty he creates with his slender hands.

Alas, I see a rose called Bess doth he enquire of my soul and heart.

Doth, he know I spied him?

My heart beats too softly for him to hear,

Yet the same time it pounds my ribcage so hard it splinters my breasts.

We pass, a smile at last!

He greats me dear Bess, I sigh.

His love for me is as strong as mine for him.

But yet we do not declare it,

For time is on our side.

I long for hot Sunday walks,

My time with him is his garden of beauty.

An Eden, of love knows no constraints,

Where sun drenched tulips open their buds and aloes heal.

Alas all good things must end, but not yet.

"Te amo dilectus meus in aeternum." *

* I love you forever my darling.

Theo's Diary, 10th September 1866

Father and I have had another argument, this morning over breakfast (it is always the same one, evolution over creation). I have done everything he has asked of me. Last year I graduated from Kings College with Theological

Studies. However, my passion lies here with the plants and the green houses. Recently I have been fanatical, reading about Charles Darwin's adventures on the Beagle.

It's hot today, normally I love the heat but my collar feels tight around my neck, oh to have the freedom to remove it. The hot house is my favourite place it has so many exotic plants. Plants that have been brought back from all over the world, places I want to see. I have dedicated all my spare time over the past three years to Kew, researching, studying and learning all I could. I can see the new students through the condensation of the glass, how exciting it must be for them. The humidity, my head.

I felt inside my pocket and brought out the two letters I have received. I stared at them as I have done all week not daring to open them. One could lead to an exciting new life and my heart's desire, whilst at the same time breaking fathers. The other would lead to a life my father and the world expects of me, but that would suffocate me. I can't bear to open them. Sweat fell from my forehead onto the letters, causing the ink to run smudging the Cape Town postmark. The bugs chirped in the heat of the day as I slowly opened the letter, my hands shook with anticipation. I felt dizzy and nauseous.

My Dear Mr Darby August 1st 1866

We were much exited to get your letter, and we would like to offer you an opportunity to work on the Kirstenbosch Botanical Gardens here in Cape Town. Your credentials speak for themselves, as do your sponsors. Arrangements will be made for you to sail from Dartmouth on HMS England due for Calcutta but please disembark at Cape Town. Further details will follow.

Yours
S. Frobershire

I read the rest of the letter, which detailed information about travel arrangements and so on. My heart was beating so fast, like distant African drums, can it be real. Can I be going to Africa? I knew what the other letter contained. It was offering me the position of Vicar for the Parish of Chertsey. I had a decision to make, I knew what my head told me to do, but my heart told me something else. Then the most exquisite dragonfly landed on my hand. I stared at it long and hard, it almost spoke to me, was it the heat, my decision was made, I was African bound.

Chapter Three, Part Two:
A Porcupine's Tale

The day started out wet and miserable. Seren did not know what to do; her friends were all busy today. She got Bess' journal down from the bookshelf and started looking through, imagining where she would end up.

As she was flicking through, she came across some pages that were stuck together, funny how she had not noticed them before. As she gently prised them open a series of pictures and postcards fell out. When she looked at them, she could see they were pictures of a place by the sea that had a strange mountain that looked like a table and a lion sitting next to it. There was also a letter addressed to Theo and a diary entry of his own, which she read. Seren wondered where this was and what it would be like to visit.

The sun had come out by now and was streaming in thorough Seren's bedroom window. It felt like a hot house. Seren was feeling pretty sleepy as she stretched and yawned. She put the journal and letter down and fell asleep. The last thing she saw before falling into a deep sleep was the porcupine quill that sat on her window ledge that she found amongst Bess artefacts.

When she awoke, she could see dragonflies dancing in the early morning sunshine. They dazzled her as the light through their wings created mini spectrums of colour all around her.

She could hear children's voices in the distance. Where was she? She wondered. As she looked up, she could see puffs of white clouds floating above a mountain with a flat top, and to the side a hill that if real would roar like thunder. She turned to look at the sea, where the children she could hear, were pulling up in a small boat. They got out of the boat and greeted Seren.

"Hello, my name is Lesedi," she looked the oldest and was about Seren's age. "This is my brother Kgosi and my sister Dalitso."

"My name is Seren; do you know where I am?" she asked.

"Our people call it Camissa (Sweet Waters) but you will know it as Cape Town," Lesedi answered.

"I was just dreaming of this place!" Seren came back.

As the children sat by the sea wondering what to do, a porcupine walked past. Seren smiled at the animal that stopped turned to Seren and said, "Hello."

A bit surprised Seren asked, "Are you well?" not knowing what else to say to a porcupine.

"Yes, quite well, thank you, are you well?" he replied.

Seren said she was very good and having a great time with her new friends.

"Your quills look amazing," Seren said.

"Yes, aren't they, sometimes they are black and white and sometimes they are white and black. They are very special as they keep me safe."

Then Porcupine turned and opened up his quill to show a magnificent display.

"Stop showing off," said Lesedi.

"Oh, OK," Porcupine said, "would you like to come for a walk with me? If you would like I will show you where I live, there you can meet Mrs Pine and all the little pines," he asked the children. So, they agreed and off they went.

They walked along the shoreline for a while until they came to a small creek running into the sea. They turned and followed the water to a row of pine trees that sat on a sandbank; just the other side was a lagoon of crystal-clear blue saltwater. As they followed the pathway around the bayou to a clearing, a waterfall sparkled as it sprinkled its fresh cooling spray into its tidal pond. Seren and Lesedi spread out their arms as they danced in the refreshing misty tiny droplets of water that quenched their thirsty bodies, while rainbows shimmered over them in the golden dappled light.

Just behind the waterfall was a small cave leading to the Porcupines home; he was waiting at the entrance. When the girls had finished, they walked through the waterfall to the other side, where Mrs Pine greeted them.

"Hello my dears," she welcomed them to her home, which was surprisingly dry and cosy with lots of dry leaves covering the ground. The little pines were fast asleep at the back of the cave but they soon stirred when they realised, they had company, and came to play with the girls. After that Mrs Pine offered them some fresh juicy watermelon to eat and they sat ready to listen to a story that Porcupine was about to tell them, a tale about his Great Ancestor who was The Gatekeeper to the Underworld.

Motsomi the Hunter

Long ago, when the land was very dry, brown and dusty Motsomi the hunter was out looking for food for his family. The land was burnt and in drought; for many years, the rains had not come and the crops had failed. Motsomi was forced to hunt far away from his village. He was tracking a lone antelope, in the heat of the day. It was time for a rest, finding a shady spot under an acacia tree he sat down.

Nearby he found a wild melon, which he peeled and ate the juicy, succulent reddish orange flesh. He then fell asleep.

When he woke, it was time for him to continue his hunt. As he started to pick up the trail of the antelope, he noticed a strange fresh print in the sandy soil. On closer examination, it was one he did not recognise. He wondered what animal the print belonged. So, he decided to track this one instead. By now the light was fading, crickets were chirping, the warm sun had started to set and he needed to find shelter as he was a long way from home. Now in the distance he could see something moving in the grass, he thought is this the animal I have been tracking? He moved closer, quietly stalking, hoping the animal would not recognise his scent. Then the animal saw him and was a little startled but carried on browsing in the long grass. The hunter was even more surprised by the strange beast. It had very short legs and a large body but very large black and white spikes protruding from its back.

"Can I help you?" the creature asked the hunter.

Not expecting the animal to talk Motsomi was a bit taken aback. So, he just replied that as he had not seen his tracks before he was inquisitive as to what they belonged to.

"It will be getting dark soon," the animal said to the hunter, "you will need shelter before the wild animals come out. Come with me and I will give you rest for tonight, if you promise not hunt me."

The hunter agreed and so he followed the animal home. Motsomi asked him what sort of creature he was.

"I am a porcupine and the Gate Keeper of the Spirit Underworld."

"I have heard of such a creature but thought you were a myth," replied Motsomi.

"As you can see, I am very real."

When they got to the place where the porcupine lived, it was a cave that led deep underground.

The entrance to the cave was low, disguised with branches and twigs. The hunter had to crouch down on his hands and knees to get in. He crawled for a little while deep underground. The entrance then opened up into a larger space, warm and dry. Some light was streaming in from above, where cracks had appeared in the cave roof. It had many leaves on the floor to make it more comfortable. Off to one side was another tunnel; it was very dark.

Porcupine said, "You must not venture down that hole it is the entrance to the underworld where the spirits of the people enter."

Motsomi asked if it was OK to make a small fire, to make some food. Porcupine said it was. He gathered some leaves he found, and by rubbing two sticks together, a fire was soon started. They both ate.

Then they slept, but hunter woke and wanted to know more about the entrance that Porcupine had told him not to enter. He followed the opening down a winding passage and in the distance; he could see a strange glowing light. As he got closer, he could see the light was coming from very tall golden yellow flowers that looked like sunshine. There were rows and rows of them giving of this light. The area before him was vast and he could see people tending their animals and villages with children playing and fields of sorghum, millet and maize growing, enough to feed many people. He could see how happy the people were and wanted this for his own family, and wondered what he could do.

Then one of the villagers saw him and asked if he was lost and could he help him. Motsomi explained his situation to him. The villager thought for a while and said that he would take him to the village elders to see if they could help.

Once they heard his plight and that of the land above the elders agreed to help the hunter. They would give him seeds from the sunflowers that he must plant these near his village they will help the other crops grow. In return, they gave him a task to do, once completed, they would give him the seeds.

In the land above was a trickster, a man called Anansi and he was causing many problems for the people when they were alive and Anansi would trick them into giving him their family stories and when that happened, the people had nothing to live for so they died. Anansi became wealthy with all the stories he had gathered and the villagers gave him much praise. He would move from village to village taking and telling stories. He would not stay at any one place for too long so people did not recognise him. The elders of the spirit world wanted this to stop and asked the hunter to capture Anansi and they would give him the seeds he needed. The elders gave him a protective spell so that Anansi could not hurt him. "You must call out to us when you need us most," they said. So Motsomi agreed.

When he went back, Porcupine was surprised to see him. "Nobody returns from the spirit world," he said.

The hunter replied, "They were not expecting me to come at this time so they let me go." He then told porcupine what they had requested of him.

After many days travelling Motsomi came across a small village where the people were very sad and in mourning. The hunter asked them why they were sad and what had happened. They told them of a stranger who came to visit, telling them wonderful stories. He then tricked them into telling him their stories and those that did had passed into the spirit world. As soon as the stranger had appeared, he then disappeared, taking with him the stories he had been told by the villagers. Motsomi told the people of his task and they wished him well for this trickster has to be stopped. The villagers fed the hunter as was the custom and off he went.

He continued on his journey until he came to the next village, by the time he arrived, it was dark and the locals were sat around the fire singing, dancing and telling stories. Amongst them was a man that did not look like he was part of this tribe. He had a group of people around him listening intently to a story, they were being told by the man. Motsomi got closer and started listening. The man was very good at telling the story and seemed to be casting a web of entrapment over the people, they were mesmerised by him. Motsomi wondered if this could be Anansi. So, the next morning the hunter asked the people of the village who this man was. They told him he was a travelling man that had just come to the village telling stories in return for shelter. Motsomi told them that he was a trickster and they must be wary of him for he will take their stories and they will die and go to the spirit world. He told them of his quest and that he had a plan to trap this stealer of stories.

That evening while the villagers were around the fire Anansi came to join them, now he said it is time for you to tell me a story. The villagers allowed Motsomi to be close to him, as he told a tale. As Anansi was telling his story Motsomi could tell that he was muttering to himself, a spell maybe. Then out of his mouth came fine silver silken threads that began to wrap themselves around Motsomi, nobody else could see this happening as they were now under Anansi spell.

The threads started to tighten themselves around Motsomi until he felt like he could not breathe anymore. Then he shouted out to the elders of the underworld to help him now, and as he did so, the threads were broken and Anansi was surprised. He started to get up to run away. As he was running, he tripped over his own threads and panicked. Motsomi was able to wrap Anansi in his own web and could now take him back to the elders in the underworld.

When he got back, the elders were very pleased to see him and what he had brought back. They unwrapped Anansi and told him they were very displeased with him for what he had done; he had made many people sad. However, if he were to change his ways, they would let him live. As storytelling was very important and he had a good way of telling them, but he must no longer steal other people's stories. People far and wide need to hear your stories. Anansi agreed to change his ways. They then turned him into a thousand smaller spiders that could roam the world telling tales.

The elders were pleased with Motsomi and honoured their promise to him. He returned to his village with the seeds from the sunflower, which he planted and tended to. They grew into the most beautiful, strong flowers ever seen. As they stood guarding Motsomi's crops, they protected them for him. Therefore, Motsomi and his family never went hungry again. And so, the story was told.

After this, it was time for the girls to leave the Pines. As they left, Mrs Pine gave Seren a gift of one of her special black and white quills to remember them by. (The quill lived on Seren's window ledge for many years.)

"Thank you for telling us about the tale and for the gift," Seren said and they parted with fond memories. Seren and Lesedi walked back to where their adventure begun.

Seren's new friends got back into their boat saying their goodbyes; she waved as she watched them sail away over the horizon. Seren sat down on the shingle and hearing a buzzing in her head, she woke. Still on her bed, she saw a dragonfly buzzing and tapping the outside of her window. She got up and went out to try and attract the dragonfly.

INDIA

Chapter Four, Part One:
India, Land of the Monsoon,
1872–1879

The left-over scent of the day's sambrani*, the evening's sweet jasmine, and the wood smoke arising, from smouldering fires, mingled and drifted sleepily on the warm midnight breeze. The stars above shone down on the rhododendron covered hills and plains that spread out before them. From magical springs on mountains high, the moon mirrored itself in the dancing fountain that cascaded into the garden pond. Alas, such magic could not mask the vast landscape of emptiness and loneliness that dispersed before me.

Theo is away at present in Fiji (he had been gone for 6months planning our next venture, as it was becoming evident that the sugar cane industry here in India was slowing and it was more profitable to grow sugar cane in other places) but he would return soon. I had plenty to attend to, the children's education, (Charles was now eight and Florence was now five) overseeing the plantation, learning about the wonders of lavender and how to grow it and use it for medicinal and relaxation purposes, which the gardener Chandra was teaching me about.

The heat is making me feel restless preventing me from sleeping. Deep in thought as I walked through the Mughal inspired nomadic garden a peacock emerged from the tulip bed whilst they slept. A high-pitched squawk (an onset to the monsoon) echoed around me as it broke the silence. The peacock plumed his startling fantail, his crowning glory into a majestical sight. A reddish-brown mongoose scuttled past, stopped, almost to speak to the peacock, a story to be told at a later time.

The garden flowed from bed to bed of Persian floral delights. The pond's evening lotus opened to illuminating moonlight rays and under the early summer stars, reflecting back a timeless dream. They caressed and floated upon the still water broken only by feeding gulping fish. Now it's time to rest ready for the celebrations to follow.

The fresh morning air woke me before the heat of the day arrived. Down below the village began to awake from its slumber, to start the business of this special day. My maid Amrita arrived to find me already awake. She prepared my bath scented with musk, sandalwood with scattered lotus petals; I slipped into its silky luxurious warm waters. After, she combed my hair and smokes the scent of sambrani through it; bringing a sense of serenity, as the brush sweeps away the negative thoughts from earlier creating a devotional atmosphere. She then rubbed sesame oil mixed with a little turmeric over my body to protect it from the sun's rays.

Amrita laid out my clothes for the day; a beautiful lime embroidered silk dress. She draped a dupatta** over my head and shoulders dappled with beautiful beads and sequins. Then she enhanced my henna tattoo for my love of Theo.

Today is the festival dedicated to the Lord Indra the deva of rainbows, thunderstorms and rain; soon it will be Monsoon season, the celebration is to honour and bless him for quenching the land of its thirst. It will be a time to dust of the dry season, a time for Good to overcome Evil.

Exquisitely painted elephant's parade in the market place, their pungent aroma mingles with that of a million herbs and spices that evokes my senses beyond their wildest imagination of a journey beyond the high hills to the escarpment below, of tales of jungles and islands of tropical delights. A time of 'tygers'*** burning bright and of lost overgrown temples with chattering monkeys and buried statues to gods no longer worshiped.

The market place is a palette of colours sounds and smells with sails of silk saris wafting and billowing gently in the breeze. Spring flowers adorn and embellish the fountain in the village square. We would drink sweet milky chai infusions of coconut and nutmeg, whilst tasting the tantalising tasty cholaar dal**** and luchi*****.

People paraded with statues and effigies of Lord Indra riding his white horse or his magnificent elephant carrying his bow of war, a gift to him. The holy men were praying, some were chanting while others were beating their drums and some throwing fresh flowers onto the ground to prepare the way for the procession.

As the afternoon brought gusty currents of air, it swirled and lifted a hue of the light spices into the air that mixed to a spectrum of yellows, golds, ambers, reds, umbers, terracottas and blues. In the excitement and frenzy, myself and Amrita's children, Harshal (Happiness) and Padma (Lotus), began to pick up handfuls of the spices and throw them in bursts at our friends and family creating an explosion of colour on our white and brown skins. We had such fun. When the excitement was over and we stopped, we looked at each other and burst into laughter. We returned home to clean up and get ready for the evening.

A sigh of relief, as evening approached bringing a friendly cooling breeze. The village below came alight as the villagers prepared for the evening celebrations. Candles and lanterns flickered from their homes while the air was infused with layers of burning fragrant oils.

We had been invited to celebrate with Amrita's family for the evening. As we arrived, we were served sweet tasting dumplings that had been soaked in honey, cinnamon and rose water. We danced and sang the evening away, then Amrita told us a tale of the monsoon.

"The foretelling of the monsoon tells us of a battle between the demon Vrita and Indra. Vrita had taken the form of a dragon that had consumed all of Earth's water. Indra vowed to kill the dragon and return water to the earth. Indra consumed soma (an immortal elixir) to attain power. A duel happened between the two. Indra triumphed, good over evil. He tore open the dragon's stomach so all the Earth's water fell back onto the land. This is why we celebrate Indra for the monsoon." ******

The evening was over and as we left the family showered us in rose petals, the smell dangled on the air as we returned home, tired but happy.

The monsoon will soon be upon us, ending this drought. The heat had been building for some time, it has become insufferable. The rains will come and then never stop, but come they must. First tiny delicate sweet raindrops fall soft and gentle, pitter-patter, on the summer gardens. The animals begin to take cover and the birds fall silent. However, fall the rain must. The clouds build softly at first, white and fluffy from the great mountains above. Darker they become with the rumblings of Lord Indra charging on his white steed, echoing around the valley, a flash of his mighty sword lights up the sky. Purple and orange the sky is on fire, the formidable heat strangles, finally the first big drops start to fall like blood out of the ever-decreasing sun's rays. A million precious jewelled drops fall from the sky every second.

The rain now falls harder and harder on tin roofs, like the sound of nails being hammered or drums constantly beaten. Ah, the relief of the cooling, warm, soaking rain. We celebrate and dance for joy as the rain jumps off the ground into the air and then settle into muddy puddles. We embrace the wonder that is the monsoon.

After weeks and weeks, it finally subsided, flooding the plains and sugar cane fields below and mingled with the salty mangrove delta way off on the horizon. The birds shook off the rain and started to sing again, as tiny animals emerge from their shelters. The summer gardens recovered their shape and vivid colours. The air is fresh to breath and the heat is abating. We settled down to enjoy the sanctuary that is autumn.

The monsoon is over.

It would not be long before we needed to leave and travel to Fiji. Theo would come back for Christmas, and then we would pack up and leave in the early spring. We had a wonderful last Christmas in India and it was good to have Theo home.

It would be hard to leave our life here and start a new one again, especially to leave Amrita. She is unable to come with us, as her parents are very old. However, we will be taking some of our workers with us and Amrita's brother, Daksh, to help us in the new plantation. We travel in the spring on the Leonardis set sail for the islands of Fiji, via Siam. Fiji has very recently become a British colony and tales of cannibalism and human sacrifice were told but also that they were a warm and welcoming race of people.

*Sambrani is a balsamic resin obtained from the bark of several species of trees. It is used in perfumes, some kinds of incense, as a flavoring, and medicine.

**Dupatta, is a long scarf that is essential to many South Asian women's suits.

***William Blake, The Tyger.

**** A traditional Bengali dish prepared from, ghee, coconut and other spices.

***** Is a deep-fried flat bread.

****** inspired by mocani.com.

Chapter Four, Part Two:
Walking with Elephant,
Peacock and Mongoose

Seren had begun a new topic in school about India; she got very excited about it. Her teacher had set her homework to write a story based on an Indian legend. Seren dug out Bess' journal as she remembered that she had spent time in India many years ago. Seren read her diary and looked at the sketches she had done. As she sat on the veranda, drinking a cool glass of apple juice with fresh apple slices, Boots the cat ran past and knocked the glass over. The apple seeds fell through the gaps in the decking, to the floor below. To her surprise the seeds started sprouting, growing shoots and stems, plants and flowers all around her which she did not recognise. Seren found herself in a tropical garden. There she could see a peacock and a mongoose in the distance. As if they were deep in conversation. This is what happened.

The day was hot and humid; Mongoose, who was called Kapil, was scuttling about the garden looking for mischief when he came across Peacock. Peacock, who was called, Sekar, was strutting his stuff as usual, displaying his magnificent feathers. Peacock and Mongoose were, friends as Mongoose kept the fateful cobra at bay, which Peacock hated. Peacock ate all the mosquitoes and bugs that Mongoose disliked because they made him scratch.

One day their good friend Elephant, who was called, Saleti, came to visit. He always admired Peacock as his feathers were so colourful and Elephant was always grey. "I wish I could look as colourful as you," Elephant said. "What can I do to be like you?"

Peacock said, "Let's go and speak to Mongoose and see what he suggests."

Mongoose pondered long and hard over Elephant's predicament and then said, "We must go and make an offering to the God of Rainbows, Lord Indra."

Elephant was very excited. "What do you think I should offer my Lord Indra?" Mongoose thought long and hard again and eventually said, "A magnificent bow." Elephant asked Mongoose and Peacock if they would help him make one.

They agreed, so over the next few days they set about making a bow that would make Lord Indra proud to use.

The three friends searched around for the best wood to use to make the bow and they came across a beautiful rosewood tree. Saleti used his trunk to pull down one of the branches, and strip it bare of leaves, which he ate of course, as they were very tasty. Kapil was able to use his sharp teeth to shape the branch into a bow shape. The wood was very pliable and able to bend at either end to create a bow.

"One thing left," said Saleti, "we need to string the bow together and then make some arrows." Sekar pulled out some of his strong beautiful tail feathers. He said the ends you can use for the arrow's quill; it will give them good flight; you can use the rest to string the bow together. So Saleti pulled the bow together while Kapil strung the two ends together. There all done. They used another couple of branches to make the bows.

When they sat back, they were pleased with what they had made. "Lord Indra will surely grant you your wish, when he sees this bow," said Kapil. After the bow was finished, they had a long journey to reach the temple of Lord Indra where they would make the offering.

Their journey started. The three friends continued walking for many days and nights to reach the temple of Lord Indra and on the way, they had many adventures. Here are but a few.

The still heat of the day was building, even the insects stopped buzzing. They decided to take a rest as the dappled rays of the golden sun broke through the lush dark green of the jungle canopy. Elephant said, "We must be very wary as this is the domain that belongs to Kamboja the Tiger." So, they took it in turns to snooze. Watching as always, even though a little sleepy himself, was a pair of amber eyes, staring at the company of three, from behind a tulip tree.

"A nice tasty peacock, with a full plume of feathers, so he won't be able to fly away. But a crafty mongoose and a huge elephant to tackle. I must be very cunning," he whispered to himself.

He disguised himself, with an old skin of an antelope and approached the three sleepy travellers.

"Where are you going?" he asked.

"We are going to visit the Temple of Lord Indra."

"But why?" Kamboja enquired.

"To make an offering of this bow!"

"It is a magnificent bow; did you make it?"

"Yes, we did," came the reply.

Then, they explained to the Tiger why they were making this long journey.

"Come with me there is a small temple near here dedicated to the Lord Indra and you must pray to him every day or you will anger him," said Kamboja.

This was true but Kamboja was planning a trap. The Tiger lead Saleti, Sekar and Kapil to the temple for them to pray.

It did not take long for them to arrive. There in a small clearing was the most beautiful temple.

The unsuspecting group started to pray. At that point Kamboja thought this was his chance so he threw off his disguise ready to pounce. But little did he know that Lord Indra was watching from above and listening to the prayers from the friends. As Kamboja was about to sink his claws into Sekar they turned and were startled.

There was a flash of light that startled the Tiger and left him dazed. At this point Sekar had enough flight in him to fly onto the back of Saleti whilst Kapil jumped and ran up his tail to safety. Saleti swung his trunk and knocked Kamboja off balance. Saleti ran like a bolt as fast as he could. When Kamboja came around the three were long gone so he stayed to lick his wounded pride.

"You can stop now Saleti," said the mongoose, "the tiger is no longer following us."

They were lucky to escape and had Lord Indra to thank.

They continued on their journey until they came to a place that belonged to a very mean and unhappy Maharaja called Rajinder Kapur. They were stopped by his soldiers.

"Where are you going?" they asked.

"We are going to visit the Temple of Lord Indra."

"But why?" the soldiers enquired.

"To make an offering of this bow!"

"It is a magnificent bow; did you make it?"

"Yes, we did," came the reply.

Then they explained to the soldiers why they were making this long journey.

They took them to the Maharaja as they were instructed to do with every stranger. They marched them through the magnificent city gate and down the main street through the busy market square into the palace grounds, and into the central court.

The Maharaja was seated on his throne and the soldiers approached him bowing as they did so. Kneeling before him they explained about the three travellers and where they were going. When the Maharaja saw the bow, he was very jealous and wanted it for himself. They said he could not have it as it was to be dedicated to Lord Indra. Then he got very angry. Now the Maharaja had a very beautiful and wise daughter the Princess Sitara and she came into the court at this moment, as she had heard of the visitors and their story.

"Be calm father," she whispered to him. She was able to sooth him with her calming voice.

She asked her father for a favour as she liked the three companions. Her favourite flower in all the land was the lotus but unfortunately it did not grow nearby, so a special trip had to be made to collect them for her. To take her father's mind off the bow she asked if they could go on to collect the lotus flowers for her. This would make them favourable in his eyes as it would please his daughter. The journey could be dangerous. They agreed but they had to leave the bow with the Princess for safe keeping, making sure that they would return. A few days later they returned with the flowers which the Princess was very grateful for and for their safe arrival.

She knew that if she made a special kind tea with the petals of the flowers her father would sleep for days and the travellers would be able to flee. So, she prepared the tea for her father which he drank, and fell into a deep sleep.

The three friends were able to make their escape with the bow. They were very thankful to the Princess for her help. She reminded them to pray to Lord Indra every day as she was a devout follower of his.

Saleti, Kapil and Sekar continued on their journey until they came across a very decorative mask in the forest. The mask was that of an Elephant's face and was to be dedicated to the God Ganesh. Saleti picked up the mask with his long trunk and put it on.

They continued walking to the next village where the women were crying in the marketplace and the men were kneeling and praying.

"What is wrong?" the friends asked the village elder.

"Our children have been taken away by an evil man to find a magic mask that he had stolen and then lost deep in the forest. He will not stop and return our children to us until it has been found," the Elder told them.

The three friends looked at each other and replied, "We have found such a mask."

But the villages did not guess, as Saleti had been wearing the mask, and they therefore did not recognise it.

"How can we help you?" Saleti asked.

"If you return the mask to him, he will let our children go, he has promised," the women cried. It seemed simple enough. The villages told them where he could be found. So, they went to see the Ahriman for that was his name which meant evil spirit.

When they found him, he asked?

"Where are you going?"

"We are going to visit the Temple of Lord Indra."

"But why?" Ahriman enquired.

"To make an offering of this bow!"

"It is a magnificent bow; did you make it?"

"Yes, we did," came the reply.

Then they explained to the Ahriman why they were making this long journey.

"But why have you come to see me?"

"We have come to see if you will release the children you have taken."

He started to get agitated. "I will not, they now belong to me, you must leave."

They asked what they needed to do to free the children. He replied by telling them about the mask.

When they revealed the mask to him his eyes lit up with great evil. The mask must have been very powerful and they wondered if they would be safe if they gave him the mask.

They told him that they were servants of the Lord Indra and if he did not guarantee their safety and that of the children, they would pray to the Lord to send a large thunderbolt and storm that would destroy him. He agreed. They then agreed a time and a place to give him the mask and release the children. In the meantime, the three prayed to Lord Indra again for help, so that they could trap the man in the mask, and make sure that he would keep his promise.

They met and the evil man let the children go as they returned the mask to him, but he forbade the three friends from leaving telling them they would be his slaves.

"Put the mask on," they said to him, "it will make you more powerful." Appealing to his vanity, Ahriman did so. As he put the mask on, he let out a terrible scream it stuck to his face, and he became trapped in the mask for all time. They took the mask back to the village; the children were already at home. The villagers said the mask belonged to the Lord Ganesh and so they placed it on the shrine in the temple that was dedicated to him.

The three travellers said goodbye to the villagers who thanked them and reminded them as they went on their way to pray every day to Lord Indra giving him thanks for what he had done for them all.

The three companions rested a while before continuing with their journey. After a few days they started walking again. The next day started out as normal, until it seemed like the sun's brightness was being turned on and off, until it finally got very dim. They three friends were not sure what was happening and became very afraid. They heard a whooshing noise and gradually it became louder and louder. They stopped and started praying to the Lord Indra to protect them and keep them safe. At that moment, they heard a loud squawk from the sky above, and then a large magnificent bird landed next to them.

"Do not be afraid of me," the bird spoke to them. "I am Garuda and I have been sent by the God Vishnu to help you on the next part of your journey."

They were startled but mesmerised by the creature that had the arms and legs of a man, the head of an eagle, a golden body with crimson wings a white face and a magnificent crown on his regal head. They greatly admired the creature.

"There is much danger up ahead and the Gods have sent me to assist you. There are creatures in the next part of the forest called Nagas. They are part human and part snake but they can change form one form to the next when needed. They are great enemies of the Gods and they contain amrita the elixir of life within their blood. If we kill them, we can make an offering of this to the Gods for a safe journey."

The three friends listened to what Garuda had to say. There is a series of waterways up ahead where the serpents live. There are also sacred wells with blessed water that the snakes keep away from. We must lure them to the wells and trap them there. Kapil the brave and clever mongoose was not afraid of snakes and was up for the challenge. Garuda thanked him for his bravery but told him these snake devils were far bigger than he had ever seen before, but he would use his trickery and that it would take all four of them to defeat them and they must use the great bow that they had made for the Lord Indra. They agreed but were feeling afraid even though protected by the Gods. He told them the Naga were three sisters. Garuda knew them from the past, as many years ago they had captured his mother. The Gods had helped him free his mother but the snakes had managed to escape. This time the Gods would allow Garuda to have his revenge.

Garuda told them the plan as they approached the waterways with care. I will fly over the waterways and flush out the snakes by flapping my powerful wings on the surface of the water. My wings will block out the sun and make the waters cold, they will not like this and will come out of the water to keep warm, and this will make them slow and vulnerable. When this happens, Saleti will charge at them to frighten them and make them unsettled, as they will not be expecting this. Then Sekar you must be ready with the arrows for Kapil to use the bow to shoot the snakes. Then you must all charge at them and guide them to the well where I will be waiting.

So, this was the plan. The great bird did what he said he would do and the sun went out and the water turned cold. The three waited for the snakes to emerge from the deep water to find warmth on the land. The three friends were horrified by their grotesque appearance. As they were finding warmth Saleti charged at the sisters who were taken by surprise and hissed at Saleti who continued to charge them. Mongoose stood up as tall and as brave as he dared and shot three consecutive arrows; each shot hitting one of the snakes. Without stopping Saleti and Kapil charged at them while Sekar flew at them opening his magnificent feathers to all their glory. They pushed them onto the wells where Garuda was waiting.

As the snakes were rounded up, they had nowhere else to go but into the well and when they saw Garuda, they hissed their poison at him, but to no avail. They fell into the well, screaming as the blessed water dissolved them. As they passed him, he was able to cut them with his powerful beak, the amrita poured out of them; Garuda was able to collect this in his mouth without swallowing it.

As he flew off, he knew the three would be safe to continue their journey. He thanked them for their help and would tell the Gods of their bravery in ridding them of one of their great enemies. In addition to getting the amrita, which would be of great benefit to the Gods, he would make an offering of it to them on their behalf, but they must not forget to pray to the Lord Indra for the rest of their journey.

One day their journey finally came to an end and they arrived at the Temple where they made their offering and sent up prayers to Lord Indra.

They knelt on the steps of the outer temple chanting a prayer proclaiming the Lord's great deeds. On entering the gates of the temple, they meditated for a while. Before entering the main temple, they cleansed their feet and hands with holy water and placed a tilak* on their foreheads. They lit candles of incense to the God, so their offering would be pleasing to him. They laid the bow on the altar, and left in reverence.

Even after all they had done, they still made Lord Indra very angry because they had not prayed to him every day. He created a mighty thunderstorm, with lightning and rain of which the three friends had never seen the like. They coward in the temple.

Then Lord Indra felt sorry for the three travellers and took pity on them by creating a rainbow to help them on their way home.

As they were passing Saleti, the Elephant walked straight through the rainbow. As he did, he was transformed, coming out the other side, magnificent as Peacock. His colours and marking were fit for any Maharaja.

The Lord Indra was still watching and when he saw Elephant in all his glory, he came to him and said, "You will be my Elephant and you will now be known as Laxman the one with lucky marks." He allowed Laxman to say good bye to Sekar and Kapil. He then rode Elephant and ascended back to the heavens.

Sekar and Kapil started the long return journey home. They were sad to start the journey without Saleti their friend. What adventures they would have on the way home?

Then every time Sekar the Peacock and Kapil the Mongoose saw a rainbow, they always thought of Saleti the Elephant and how proud of him they were. They pondered on what great adventures he would be up to with Lord Indra, they hoped that he was now happy and felt fulfilled.

Seren woke from her long dream. She realised that her apple juice had spilled, so she cleaned it up. After that she wrote the story down, using Bess' drawings for inspiration. She hoped her teacher would like the tale.

* A mark worn by a Hindu on the forehead to indicate caste, status, or sect, or as an ornament.

THAILAND

Chapter Five, Part One:
Land of Smiles

Leaving India for Fiji, Stop at Siam (Now Thailand), 1879

It was a sad day leaving India, the friends we had made and especially Amrita and her family. She watched us and wept as we waved goodbye and left the dockside. I wish she could have come with us. However, I understand her wish to remain.

The voyage past uneventfully; and the time was spent pondering on what had been and what may follow. We were to stopover in Siam for a short stay to collect passengers, goods and migrant workers for our new venture in Fiji.

We had been invited to stay with Sir Thomas Knox the British Consul-General and his wife in Bangkok. However, when we arrived, his daughter and son-in-law greeted us. His son-in-law was Louis Leonowens*, the son of Anna Leonowens*. Louis had returned to the country some years earlier, to marry Sir Thomas Knox's daughter and to become a Captain in the King's Royal Cavalry.

We were taken to the consul residence and made to feel welcome. The building was ornately decorated with and had vast gardens. Our rooms overlooked an inner courtyard with a golden fountain in the centre, decorated with elephants, tigers and monkeys. Our workers were housed within the grounds in the servant quarters, the men and their families were well looked after. We had about forty with us and were due to take another thirty from Siam to work on the sugar plantation in Fiji.

Over the next few days, we were treated to some of the exotic sites that Bangkok had to offer with our hosts Louis and Caroline. Visiting temples, markets and even a shadow puppet show.

The day started with a journey to a Buddhist temple. The temple was golden and heavenly, Nirvana on earth a sanctuary from the heat and humidity. Leading to the temple was an intricate waterway system carved out with blue stone in the shape of a lotus. While on top of the water floated lotus petal, giving of a delicate scent. Steps lead us to four stone dragons that guarded the entrance to the temple. The head monk was there to greet us he held his palms together and bowed; we returned the gesture. Then we removed our shoes, as it was traditional in India too, before we entered the prayer hall. There in front of us a statue of Buddha, the heavy scent of jasmine infused incense filled the hall. People were asking for enlightenment through their devotional prayers. We walked around the statue and felt comforted that he was watching over us. We left bowing as we backed away from Buddha's statue not turning our back on him until we were outside of the great hall.

The markets places were set on the river and were buzzing with activity; the market sellers or blue shirts, as they were named, rowed their boats up and down the river selling everything from fruits and vegetables, to spices, to fabric, to birds in cages and sticky rice and dumplings, to eat. The avenue of market stalls lit by many lanterns lead off from the riverbank into a maze of endless shops and sweet smells that floated on the evening breeze.

The next day a jungle trek on elephants. Through twisted jungle vines and along muddy rivers to villages beyond the city. On our return to the city, a festival of masks and dancers revelled in the streets of Bangkok.

Our last day, a visit to one of the great shadow-puppet shows, the evening was humid and sultry, broken only by the occasional breeze of heavy incense rising on the night air. We were treated to a spectacular night of dance and shadow, the struggle between good and evil and of love and betrayal. The stage was set outside in the dusky light as thousands of candles, in coconut shells, flickered like the stars in the night sky. The musicians started to play, strange and beguiling music from the orchestra that was seated on the floor between the stage and us. Narration was in the form of song, and was in Siamese so we did not understand much of what was sung, but the shadow puppets spoke for themselves. The play depicted Rama descending to earth on his chariot. Where he meets his wife Sita. Rama's evil brother who has disguised himself tricks and captures her. For a time Sita is seduced by the brother. The brothers fight and Rama is almost defeated when Hanuman his friend comes to his rescue. They defeat Rama's brother and Sita and Rama are reunited. Buddha then descends to take Rama and Sita back to the heavens and peace returns to the earth.

As the show was coming to the end, I became very feverish and flustered and passed out due to the heat. I was rushed back to our apartment, where the doctor came to examine me, only to discover that I was pregnant. Not planned and not good timing, but welcome news. The journey to Fiji was postponed for a few days while I regained my strength ready for the onward journey.

We re-boarded the Leonardis. As we left Siam, the sun setting in the distance, little did we know what was to lie ahead. The journey was long and hard, the wind and picked up and the seas were choppy. We had brought typhoid, sickness and death, aboard the ship. I helped nurse as many as I could but we lost half to the illness and they were buried at sea. A heart-breaking time as we considered our workers as family. Amrita's brother amongst them, how was I to write to her and let her know.

*Anna Leonowens was an Indian-born British travel writer, educator and social activist, fictionalised in Anna and the King of Siam.

Land of Smiles

The heart of the Lotus bursts open,
Purity fills the air with golden scent.
All hail to the jewel in the lotus as candles flicker with
devotion,
Calmness arises from the temple of dawn where once we
dreamt.

A festival of ghosts, masks bright and colourful,
Line a patchwork of rice husks and coconut leaves.
To the return of the prince, the ghosts of Phi Ta Khon so
cheerful,
Dance and parade with bells on their sleeves and heels.

To floating night time canal markets busy and vibrant,
Blue shirts sell their goods as fireflies flit on wing.
Dragons fruit glows in the moonlight with a lingering
pineapple fragrance,
As canoe, cooks steam mango sticky rice and dumplings.

Spicy jungle trek deep lush and tangled,
Bamboo houses next to winding muddy red rivers.
Iconic elephants roam through poppy fields and jungle
jangle,
Dizzy height to golden spiritual flags and heavenly figures.

Mystical hanging islands with lost temples of gold,
Luxury awaits with embroidered silken sarong.
To tell the tale, of Anna and her king, Siam of old,
In a dance of hope the Isan Bantheong.

We celebrate the full moon,
As we send sky born lanterns to light the night sky.
The balance of nature is in harmony,
With the Spirits of the land.

Giant hornbill wings echo above the vast forest,
As lilies fragrant the lagoons.
We dedicate offerings to the water Goddess,
As we cross a bridge to the spirit world.

Fluorescent coral, its glory seen by few,
As sea monkeys float by on a carpet of yellow sunflowers.
A land in peace and alliance with nature,
Where the painted butterfly bat glides free.

SAWATDEE

Chapter Five, Part Two:
Hanuman the Monkey God

Seren had been looking at shadow puppets and masks for her drama lesson, she was keen to find out where they came from. Her homework was to write her own version of a play. After watching 'The King and I', she realised they had their origins in old Siam now Thailand. She remembered that Bess had visited Siam on her way to Fiji. Seren went to find Bess journal for inspiration. She was not disappointed and even though Bess was only there for a short time she got to do some exciting things like visiting temples and watching shadow puppet plays.

Here is a tale Seren wrote through the use of shadow puppets, masks and dance. The play is about courage and bravery where the actors portrayed different Gods through their avatar animals.

The Play

The stage was set, a curtain of evening stars and a bright shining moon parted, lighting a silver pathway.

As the curtains opened the narrator moved onto stage, wearing a monkey mask, he positioned himself at centre front stage.

"I am Hanuman the Monkey God and I will tell you a tale of the birth of my people and of a great battle we had against the Tiger God Baghashwar; he, who runs through the forest."

As he continued narrating, the actors began dancing and performing allowing his words to come alive. Musicians added ambience to the show, by playing their instruments the Khong Wong Yai (gonged), the Saw Sam Sai (bowed) and the Taphon (drum).

"One evening while out walking," the narrator continued, "a young Princess Yu-Phin came across an exquisite flower, one she had not seen before. Shaped like a star that had fallen from the sky. It glowed a translucent, brilliant lilac colour, its scent of sweet amber with hints of warm nutmeg spice and essence of lotus."

The actress playing Yu-Phin danced across the stage, picked up the flower. She lifted it to her nose to absorb its scent. As she looked closer, the flower opened to reveal a tiny but fully formed baby monkey.

"The girl took this to be a gift from the Gods and took the monkey, who she called Anurak, meaning Angel, home to care for it," Hanuman continued.

The set behind changed to the girl's home. A large house on the Chao Phraya River.

"Some time had passed and Yu-Phin was older. The monkey and girl grew closer and became inseparable friends."

The two friends entered the stage, and started a game together; they then had a pretend tea party and danced together.

"One day, the girl decided to make a mask of the monkey, she spent many days making it, which she then painted and decorated. I, Hanuman, was so impressed with her that I decided to pay her a visit."

As the actor, playing Hanuman moved off stage day became evening.

From above the Monkey God came down on a moonbeam sprinkled with the same flowers Yu-Phin had found earlier. He hovered above her.

She gasped and bowed before him; she rose up then danced in his presence.

"Do not be afraid," I am the God Hanuman he announced to her. "I am greatly dazzled by the mask you have made; it is in great honour of me. I would like you to make more and in return I will bless you, with your heart's desire."

The narrator returned to the heavens and then reappeared on stage to continue telling the story. The Princess set to the task of making the masks.

So, time passed, and she made many masks, all highly painted and decorate. It had taken many years and now the girl was a woman. Her devoted Anurak would watch her constantly, while she created the masks.

When Hanuman returned, he was so happy with Yu-Phin, that as promised, he blessed her by giving her, her heart's desire, a man to love. Hanuman changed her companion, Anurak, into a handsome Prince, whom she later wed. Anurak placed a sindoor* on Yu-Phin as a sign of his everlasting love.

He said, "This is my son, Anurak, whom you have cared for, shown devotion to and loved unconditionally all this time," Hanuman spoke to Yu-Phin.

Now Hanuman took all the masks as he had a plan for them. He transformed them all into living monkeys that became his people. Now there were many actors on the stage with monkey masks on. They danced, got up to mischief, stole fruit from the market stalls and climbed across buildings into homes. However, the humans did not seem to mind this as they thought it would bring them luck; they celebrated them as a gift from the Gods.

Some years later, the Princess now grown, had married Anurak.

"One day while the Princess and her husband had gone to the forest to hunt tigers," Hanuman recited to the audience, as the scene was behind him was changed.

The scene now changed to a forest backdrop with a hidden ruined temple. The actress playing Yu-Phin entered the stage.

"Yu-Phin had decided to go for a walk in the forest, when she came across a ruined temple, she could see that it was dedicated to me, the Monkey God," Hanuman continued the narration.

As she felt safe, she continued on her walk knowing that Hanuman would look after her. In the overhanging trees and vines, she could see many monkeys playing, grooming, feeding and chattering away. But soon they started to get agitated and their chattering became an alarming call that warned Yu-Phin danger was ahead. She started to run and as the monkeys got louder and louder, she panicked, lost her way and fell over a crooked tree root.

At that point, a man prowled onto the scene wearing the mask of a tiger, the audience gasped. He danced and slinked his way sniffing the air, the monkeys went silent. Yu-Phin was trapped and could not move.

"I am Baghashwar the Tiger God, and you are my prisoner," the Tiger roared. Yu-Phin was very afraid and wept. "Be gone," he shouted, to the monkeys and they scattered.

Now Hanuman had seen this, it made him sad and angry. Baghashwar was his great enemy and of his people. He set out to save the Princess. He gathered his army and sent them out to defeat the Tiger God and rescue the Princess.

Their armies met and there was a great battle. The scene changed again. Lightning struck and thunder boomed (from behind the set) as the monkeys and tigers clashed. There was lots of commotion on the stage; there were many actors, (mainly children who did the acting and fighting in the form of silat pattani**) wearing tiger and monkey masks. The monkeys were sharp tricksters while the tigers were cunningly sly. The battle raged for some time until the two Gods entered, the battle became fierce. They clashed in the sky, and bright sparks flew around them. However, the monkeys were more intelligent and greater in number and eventually the tigers grew tired and became subdued. Hanuman's army was triumphant and they were able to save the Princess and reunite her with Anurak.

Baghashwar disappeared deep into the jungle to lick his wounds and plan his next manoeuvre to defeat his enemy Hanuman and his people.

After that when Yu-Phin and Anurak returned home they built a new temple dedicated to Hanuman their saviour. Every year on the anniversary they would go to the temple and make a special offering to Hanuman to thank him for saving the Princess.

The End

Seren was happy with what she had written and gave the homework in. Seren's teacher enjoyed the play so much that she allowed Seren and her friends to perform it in a later lesson.

*Red pigment made from powdered red lead, especially as applied as a dot on the forehead or in the parting of the hair of married Hindu women.

** a type of martial arts dance.

FIJI

Chapter Six, Part One:
Fiji – The Coral Coast

Fiji, 1879–1882

It was 3 months to the day since we arrived in Sigatoka on the Leonardis (carrying Indian and Siamese migrant workers for the new sugar plantations) from Calcutta*. We initially stayed with John Smith-Williams, a family friend, and owner of the first banana plantation on Fiji. The banana plantation was a welcome sanctuary after the time at sea. Due to the typhoid outbreak on board the ship. My baby is due shortly.

I am still missing India, Amrita, her family and the devastating loss of her brother. Nevertheless, Litiana, our new maid had made us feel safe and welcome. Fiji, had suffered its own losses recently as we had come to land on deserted beaches due to the recent war and measles epidemic. Both a few years earlier, had decimated the indigenous population.

We had come to this jewelled isle with a dark history. There was still evidence of shipwrecks and of part buried cannibal ovens. However, its beauty outshone any past darkness that enveloped it. To me this was Elysium** on earth. A lush green island full of tree ferns, palms, crystal blue waters, hidden waterfalls, vibrant colourful plants, birds and fruit. I would never find a place that I was so free than here in Fiji, my very own paradise. The tranquillity captivated my heart, the islands called to me, evoking all my senses. Fiji's magic had cast her spell of enlightenment over me.

Every morning as I wake from my slumber, the fresh sea breeze, salty and sweet, hits my lips as it coasts through palm trees rooted at the water's edge. I turn, but Theo has already awoken and left for the plantation. The early morning freshness mingles with the island's pungent, hushed, volcanic tones. I hear the waves rumble over the distant coral reef, a comforting sound. Pale lavenders, pinks and greys hover over the horizon, as the sun rises, they calmly merge into a pale cyan morning sky. Ripe citrus and floral fumes from the frangipani drift through the open window. Time to rise and take my morning walk. Our chalet was a stone's throw from the beach, near the village of Sigatoka. I would stroll along the shingle barefoot to feel the sand between my toes. Then Litiana would call me for breakfast. She would bring me a bowl of exotic fruit of moli kana, nia dama and kavika***, to invigorate my taste buds.

After the morning chores, the early bright aroma was overtaken by the afternoon's baked heat. The sun-drenched wood of the chalet creaked and groaned as we sat on the veranda overlooking the sea. The deep azure sky reflected in the turquoise sea with its white horses racing to shore. The hint of ylang and ginger wafted achingly slowly, on the moist air. As the heat subsided, the chalet would let out a sigh of relief. Sometimes, there was a stillness before a tropical storm arrives. The sky and sea would darken, a crack of distant thunder, the wind would rise up followed by intense rainfall. We quickly shut up the windows and shutters, the wind was exhilarating. Then as soon as it had arrived, it would be gone, leaving blue skies, a freshness and glistening green leaves. We have yet to feel the full force of a cyclone, pray we never do!

The evening comes; a buttery caramel smell with dreamlike undertones is dispersed over the islands, from the heavily scented, potent flowers. The sound of the roosting birds is replaced by the intense chirping and croaking of the night insect and frogs. In contrast, the geckos, silent and deadly lay in secret awaiting their prey.

Theo returns silently too, after his day at the plantation, in time for a delicious supper of coconut, fish and yams, prepared by Litiana. We sit on the veranda watching the sun go down with its intense fiery scarlet and burnt orange sky topped by an opal blue aurora. It creates indigo silhouettes of the palm trees, as they sway themselves slowly to sleep, with the ever-present sound of the waves crashing over the barrier. Still distant, but now deadly luring, with the knowledge that sharks swarmed on the other side of the safe lagoon.

The Plantation

After breakfast, sometimes, I would go with Theo to the plantation to help feed the workers their lunch. The plantation was situated about two miles away up river. We walked to the riverside, where we would clamber onto the narrow wooden boats. Malakai and Tevita two locals would paddle us up stream. The river was wide and muddy and the dense forest foliage cradled the riverbanks. Here it was still dense but further up it had been cleared for the plantation. As well as the sugar, Theo had planted sandalwood shrubs known as

Yasi to the locals. They had been over harvested here in the early part of the century and were now almost gone on the island. Theo used them to surround the plantation; they gave of a warm woody scent, and would be good for producing oil. The yellow-coloured wood was also valuable too. However, the shrubs were slow growing so the crop would take a while to yield any value. After lunch, the workers would go back to work but Theo and I walk to a nearby waterfall to cool off. We would follow a small tributary from the river, away from the plantation, back into the native bush, clambering over moss-laden rocks and tree roots. The forest opened up to an abundance of ferns and orchids. We would sit for a while, as the sun shone through the filigreed canopy of trees, we watched and listened to the many parrots and lorikeets flying from tree to tree. Then we would undress and swim in the warm waters of the small pool, the waterfall dived into. The rainbow dappled water made our skin feel soft and smooth. Glittering drops of pure tropical relaxation. Time had no meaning here, it made me feel so alive. After our swim, we would dry in the warm sun, dress and return to the plantation.

Sometimes we would return home on horseback. The plantation horses were called Cagi (Wind) and Wai (Water). We would follow the river back until we got to the beach, and then let the horses cool off in the sea where the palm trees would gently bend in the breeze to greet the sea. Occasionally, we would pass locals on their way home, with machetes, after they had climbed and gathered their coconuts. 'Bula' they would greet us with their enriched golden-brown skin and pure white teeth (due to their diet).

Litiana's Village

Today we took taking Litiana back to her village as it is a special celebration day. We have been invited as quests. The village was set on high ground surrounded by small ponds, which had been diverted from the nearby river.

To the outskirts were fields of yams, cassava and taro. Their houses were built on stilts, still quite primitive, with high thatched roofs made of dried grasses. Inside the wooden structures the walls and floors were made of large woven mats, with highly decorated wall hangings made of tapa. There were small open windows, will pull down shutters made from woven flax. The furniture was simple as they mainly sat on the floor and slept on straw and raffia mats.

Litiana's family who spoke only a little English greeted us warmly as they welcomed us into their home. They were busy with preparations for the celebration and the feast. Their cooking was done outside in large clay pots over open fires or lovo deep with the ground, where the food is wrapped in leaves from the taro.

The women here wore even more explicit clothing here than in India, where they exposed their midriffs. In Fijian villages the women still were topless. They wore skirts made of intricately decorated tapa and woven grass. On such occasions they made garlands of flowers that they wore on their head, called tekiteki and around their wrists and ankles. Litiana presented me with one. It was made from frangipani, hibiscuses, lotus and ylang-ylang, I will treasure it forever.

In the centre of the village was a large open sided meeting building where the villages would gather on such occasions to celebrate. We all sat here in a circle and ate the delicious food that had been prepared. Then we drank kava a drink made from the local pepper plant that had been pounded. It was mixed with water and served in a coconut shell or tanoa bowl. It made your lips and tongue tingle when you drunk it. The evening was followed by dancing, chanting and clapping. As you can imagine we stayed the night and returned home the next day.

A Letter from Ma and Pa

A letter had arrived from ma from South Africa; the post took over six months to arrive. Two came together. The first was about a war that was brewing between the Zulu King and the British but under the pretext of troubles between the Zulus and the Boers over border disputes. Ma thinks it will all blow over. The second letter detailed the war had got worse and there were battles at Isandlwana and Rorke's Drift. The whole legion had been wiped out at Isandlwana. A devastating result for the British. However, they did not take to it lightly. No sooner that the war had begun it was over. The Zulu King was left a fugitive after the battle of Ulundi and the Zulu army dispersed.

*Now Kolkata.

*** Elysium, an Ancient Greek paradise.

**Pomelo, orange coconut, rose apple.

Fiji – The Coral Coast

I awoke to the sound of the waves waxing and waning over the brittle coral reef, salt mingled with the heavily perfumed hibiscus. Coconuts spilling sweet milk as they cracked the hard ground below. From the kitchen, came the smell of zinging tea freshly plucked and brewed that refreshed my taste buds. The sea was calling to me as it rolled and crashed over the living rocky barrier.

The chalet, our home for these past months, was simple and uncluttered in its presence, natural and clean, curtains blowing in the warm morning breeze. Left over aromas of ash from the night before, mingled with morning fresh vegetation. Friendly geckos chirped and scuttled off to their daily hideaways, under raffia mats and exotic masi wall hangings with patterns of turtles.

I rose and dressed. The wet warm sand beckoned, sharp and tingling mixed with sand dollars that had drifted on dreamy ocean tides to land on deserted beaches. Blue starfish beneath my feet their underbellies naked and exposed. Sch, Sch, Sch the tide back and forth, back and forth. I sat under a shady splayed traveller palm out of the golden sun, on a deserted beach to rest, drifting into a narcotic sleep.

I was woken by the sound of sweet singing coming from afar; the music was strange and bewitching. The orange sun was now setting over the pink violet horizon. White horses galloped at the sea edge in the cooling evening current. Just as the sun drifted slowly below the horizon, the sea was now soft and passive once again.

I followed the enchanting sound as it called to me. A haunting ukulele joined, as the swaying palm trees danced in melodic rhythm. Villagers packed away paw-paw and cassava from their market stalls. The smell of baked bread still lingering on the air. Time for home. I passed dense organic growth, sugar cane and banana plantations. Tomorrow a cascading waterfall beckons with parrots and lorikeets chirping from the jungle interior.

Chapter Six, Part Two:
The Song of the Sea

The family had been to see South Pacific at the theatre, in Torquay. When they got home Seren dug out Dad's old record of the film and started listening to it on her new record player. She was singing along to 'Happy Talk', whilst reading Bess' diary of her time in Fiji. She found herself reading of turtles, dolphins, coral reefs, tropical beaches and mystical pacific islands.

A small wall-hanging made of tapa*, decorated with a picture of a sea turtle, fell from the diary. Seren found a space on her wall to put it on.

"Happy talking happy talk, you've got to have a dream, if you don't have a dream how you gonna have a dream come true**," Juanita Hall's voice echoing in the background.

She must have then fallen asleep to the magical and enchanting Bali Hai, "Come to me Bali Hai, lonely island lost in a foggy sea, come to me Bali Hai, special island**," she seemed to be calling out in her dream of the tropics.

She awoke to find herself in a place similar to the one she had been reading about. She stood gazing at a secret waterfall cascading into a great pool, surrounded by dense lush forest; the cooling spray sprinkled her face. A green parrot, squawking emerged for the thick, undergrowth of purple bougainvillea and ivy. The sound of the tropical jungle rustled around her. The pool looked inviting as she sat beside it, gingerly submerging her feet. A paw-paw, fell from a tree, its succulent juice satisfied her growing thirst, as she ate it.

A tattooed boy with deep brown eyes and a bright smile emerged from the trees and came towards her; Wasiu (meaning Song of the Sea) was his name.

"Bula," he greeted Seren with a flash of his perfect white teeth. "Would you like to go swimming with the dolphins?" he asked as he reached out his hand, which Seren took.

"Don't be afraid," he said as he helped Seren through the forest and over rocks to the beach below. He was very strong and Seren felt safe with him. Seren admired the tattoos on his arms. They were of traditional shapes mixed with shells on the crest of a wave.

"Did your tattoos hurt?" Seren asked the boy.

"Yes, but I was brave," he replied. They arrived at the beach.

Walking over the rock pools the salt popped as it evaporated in the heat of the sun. As they reached the watery edge, he broke into song.

"Qalo me mi (Swim to me),
Makawa vonu (Ancient turtle),
Na cava me tai (Come to shore),
Telk keola ena ganisici iesutale (Take us on shell back),
E taucoko na wasa (Across the sea),
Me koula baravi (To golden sands),
Na yanuyanu ni babale (The island of dolphins),

Kei-na sisili me baleta na kena (And dive for pearls). Ena titobu karakarawa wasa (In the deep blue sea). Me lesutale ena na kala ni matanisiga (To return at the setting sun)."

Then two turtles appeared, heads bobbing above the crested blue sea, their large black eyes beckoned. The two friends climbed onto their smooth patterned shelled backs. They friends were of an intricate design just like the boy's tattoo. Black and brown they were made up of convex diamond shapes, scratched and worn in places, the homes of these ancient sea creatures.

The turtles swam, flippers flicking cool spray into their faces. The barrier beyond beckoned, with its coloured coral, iridescent fish and friendly dolphins, deep beyond the world above.

Seren and Wasiu spent the day swimming with the Spinner dolphins, lying on the sun-drenched beach, on the sacred island of Kadavu, where the turtles lived. Wasiu would occasionally dive down, to a sunken world, where the giant clams were found. To look for pearls for Seren, which he then strung into a necklace.

Just as the large, blood red sun was setting over the horizon, the sky turned from oranges into a haze of golden purples silhouetting the palm trees. The two children were beginning to get hungry so Wasiu said it was time to go back to his village for some food, dancing, music and storytelling. They climbed back onto the turtles who took them back to the main island near to Wasiu's village.

When they arrived, they could see the village all lit up and the smoky smell of the food coming from the lovo***, that the women had prepared. This tantalised their taste buds.

They said goodbye to the turtles and thanked them for a lovely day and for looking after them, Wasiu blessed them, as they swam away, to guide them on their way home.

It was a very warm evening and Seren changed into some traditional clothing that Wasiu's mum had given her. It was a bit scratchy, as it was made out of tapa cloth, but highly decorated with hibiscus flowers it went well with the necklace Wasiu had made for Seren. His sisters, put colourful leis of sweet-smelling perfumed hibiscus and frangipane flowers around her neck and wrists. Seren and Wasiu sat with the family and watched the dancing. The women danced the fan dance followed by the men with their spear dance. The music and singing that followed evoked a natural awareness in Seren; she felt a connection with nature and freedom she had not felt before. Seren was having such a good time.

Finally, the food was ready. When the lovo was unwrapped from the banana leaves the steam cleared. Seren could see the tender pork surrounded by sweet potatoes and other vegetables she did not recognise. They sat, and all the food was shared. Then the storytelling started, by one of the old women of the village. Seren was ready for a story to back up the rawness of the singing.

The Giant and the Spirit of Fire

"Long before our ancestors arrived by boats, giants roamed these islands. The giants knew about fire and were afraid of it, as they were not able to control it. The fire was wild, spurred on by the warm winds that blew it was out of control. Then one day one of the giants went in search of the source of the fire. He sailed to a neighbouring island with a large volcano at its centre. As he climbed, he prayed to the Gods to give him strength to complete his task.

Halfway up, he stopped to take a rest. He was joined by a lizard with a bright red tongue, who asked what he was doing. The giant explained.

You have come to the right place. If you do something for me, I will help you. I have been trapped on this island for many years and I cannot escape on my own, replied the lizard.

The giant agreed to help. *What do you need me to do?*

I need you to collect an item from the bottom of the ocean. In a large blue clam, you will find a bottle that contains a liquid potion, please return it to me. Beware; there lives a sea monster, that you will need to defeat, it protects the clam and its contents. Then with a swish of his tail a spear appeared next to the lizard. *Take this spear to help you defeat the monster,* the lizard instructed the giant.

The giant returned to the shore, and swam out to the deep sea. He easily found the clam, as it shone an iridescent bright blue against a grey rock, but it closed tight as the giant approached. He prized it open. Inside, as the lizard said, was a bottle; which he put it safely into his belt. Just as he was about to swim back, he caught sight of the sea monster.

It approached with such speed emerging from a dark cave. Its fluorescent purple scales flashed creating electrical waves as it moved towards the giant. From side to side, it swam its forked, squid tail flipping behind it. As it got closer, the giant could see its eyes, a menacing black, as cold as the cave it appeared from. Two threatening horns upon its head with jaggered teeth protruded from its jaws, the giant was confident in his strength.

The nearer the creature got the faster it propelled itself. The giant poised himself to take the full impact. The monster hit him with all his might, taking the giant's breath away; he gulped, but regained his form. The monster tried to bite the giant's neck upon impact with his powerful teeth. The giant held the monster at bay. They wrestled, their grip on each other tightened. Then the sea monster whipped his tail and caught the giant by surprise, who dropped the spear in the struggle. The giant changed his grasp to try and break the monster's thick neck. To no avail, both fell to the sea bottom where they continued their battle. The giant losing air from his large lungs struggled to hold his breath, he needed to react quickly.

Then the monster flashed with electricity, loosened its grip, and the giant managed to break free. Some respite, as he swam away. Pursued by the monster, the giant spied the spear below. It was stuck in a rocky crevasse, glowing, he grabbed hold of it. The giant had lost sight of the monster, where was it? He looked around; just as the monster came towards him from above. The creature was almost upon him, the giant turned at the last moment to reveal the spear. The monster had no time to divert his course; it swam right into the spear. The giant had speared the creature's heart. There was one last almighty flash of light from the monster, the ocean shuddered, the creature was dead. The giant, exhausted, swam back to shore and re-climbed the volcano, where he returned the bottle to the lizard, who drunk its contents.

At moment that, the lizard transformed into a pure golden fire spirit. *This is my true form, do not fear me.* He glowed and burnt magnificently, the giant was not afraid and felt safe in his presence.

I am the good spirit of fire. My evil brother who wants to spread death and destruction by fire throughout the islands trapped me here. As you have helped me escape, I will teach you how to control fire, to be able to fire walk on white coals, dance with the fire and cook lovo. The lizard did as he promised and gave him the secrets of how to control fire. The giant now full of this knowledge begun his journey home.

When he returned home, the people were pleased with his wisdom. Therefore, they made him their lord, as he was able to subdue the raging fire.

Over time the giants disappeared into myth and laid down to sleep to form the many islands we now call home."

After the story the old woman sang a sweet lullaby, Seren fell asleep as the song went on.

She woke, rubbing the smoke from her eyes from the dying fires embers. In the distance, she could hear a voice calling her. It was coming from the shoreline. As she rose and got closer, she could tell the caller was distressed. In the moonlight, Seren could see a turtle calling to her, "Seren,

Seren, Seren." The sound mesmerised her like the waves drifting onto the sandy beach.

"Can you help me please?" the turtle asked.

"Of course, what's the matter?"

"It's my children they need help. Climb onto my back, I will take you to them."

Seren did what she was asked, the turtle used her flippers to push them off from the beach into the water, and off they went.

"I had to leave them on a small island not far from here, they should be hatching. There were firewalkers on the island and it has now caught fire, and they will be cut off from the sea, unless we can rescue them," the turtle told Seren.

"There is a secret lagoon, known only to us turtles, it is a safe way onto the island, but we will have to swim under the coral to get to it. Hold your breath, here we go," the turtle said as they went under.

As they dived Seren held tight, they came up in the safety of the lagoon, Seren gasped for air. Seren could see the smoke rising from the fire, creating a blood red mist across the horizon.

"Cloud fire," said the turtle, "quick, you must hurry."

Seren made her way through the forest to the beach. The fire was raging, with the heat and the smoke, she began coughing, and she tied a piece of her skirt around her nose and mouth, to help her breathe.

The turtles had begun to hatch by the time Seren got to them. Seren scooped the little ones up in her skirt and she made her way hastily back to the lagoon. There she reunited mother and babies. Safe in the lagoon they all swam off.

The mother, who was eternally grateful, took Seren back to Wasiu and his home. Wasiu, by this time was getting worried but he was pleased to see her.

Wasiu sung Seren a final song, the Isa Lei the song of farewell. He said his heart would yearn for her; they hugged their goodbyes and he gave Seren a sand dollar**** to remember him by.

Beep, beep, beep the alarm went off, too good to last, time for school. Once last look at the turtle wall-hanging before Seren left for school, wishing she could go back to sleep and dream of further adventures with Wasiu and his friends the dolphins and turtles. She thought she got a smile from the turtle, but it was only a reflection of a sand dollar that had just appeared on her window ledge. How did that get there? Seren thought.

"Hurry up Seren or you will miss the school bus," Mum called from downstairs.

*The bark of the paper mulberry tree, cloth made used in the Pacific islands.

**Rodgers and Hammerstein from South Pacific.

***this is the Fijian name for a feast cooked in the earth.

****a flattened sea urchin which lives partly buried in sand.

AUSTRALIA

Chapter Seven, Part One: Dreamtime

Australia, 1882–1885

The HMS Dart took 11 days to sail from Fiji to Cairns. Our new home for the past few months had been Smithfield a small settlement just north west of Cairns. The native forest had been cleared, ready for the plantation that was to be situated between Smithfield and Kuranda.

We decided to leave Fiji after there was unrest with the local native mountain tribes. There was also trouble brewing on some of the other plantations, due to the way the Indian workers were treated. The situation in places was beginning to become unpleasant. Theo was always fair with our workers; they were more like family to us. After we decide to leave, some of them said they wanted to come with us, while others decided to return home to India. They were free men and women, after all.

John Smith-Williams who had become our closest of friends and ally in Fiji, was about to start a new banana plantation in Australia. John knew how Theo worked and offered him the position of Plantation Manager. There had been a population growth in Australia. The discovery of gold in Northern Queensland, on the Palmer River, brought an influx of immigrants, especially from China. The demand to grow food was high. The miners would return from inland to the coastal areas and Cairns. The Cavendish bananas were grown in greenhouses in England arriving in Australia via Fiji.

Therefore, we came and Litiana accompanied us. Her parents had died in the measles epidemic and she had no family of her own.

Close by there were many tea plantations in operation, these were new to Queensland too; ours was one of the first banana plantation in this area. The weather and conditions in the Australian rainforest were similar to that of India. With my knowledge, I had gained from my time living in India I started to grow a variety of lavender plants. They grew very successfully here. With the help of Litiana, I started making soaps, basic beauty products and essential oils with the lavender. There was a local market in the town of Kuranda so we would go there to sell the products. There was talk of them building a trainline from Cairns to Kuranda that would make life easier. That would be a great engineering feat. (We heard later the line was started in 1885 and completed in 1890).

An Australian Christmas

Over the years, I have celebrated Christmas differently according to the country I was livening in at the time, very much depending on the local customs and food available to us.

In South Africa, I remember ma kept many traditions from the old country, especially her plum pudding. In India and Fiji, Christmas was very different but we always decorated the house. Here in Australia, we would bring in a fluorescent yellow flowering tree called a Moodjar, not that the place needed brightening up with the bright sunshine. The tree had great sacred and spiritual meaning to the local tribes, so naturally it became our new Christmas tree.

Of course, the build-up to the special day was always extra busy, preparing food and planning events. All the local plantations and farmers would gather together and share the day. Large tents were erected by the men and the women would then decorate the tables. Litiana and I spent many hours making damper bread, biscuits, jams and chutney using such things as quandong, a native peach with a tart-bitter sweet taste. I also made ma's plum pudding, one tradition I kept.

On the day, we would briefly go to church, return home and open presents as a family. Then we would meet up with the other local plantation and farming families and their workers. Such a large spread of food was put on for all. The men prepared chicken and pork roasting them on spits over large tin barrels.

After lunch, there were games, races and even a game of polo that the Indian migrants had brought with them from India.

At the end of the day, we were all well fed and very tired.

Boxing Day morning was spent relaxing. In the afternoon, a cricket match had been organised between the workers and a team that Theo had picked. It was a great day, apart from making all the sandwiches and the humidity. The match was very close, but eventually there was a winning team, and to great relief it was Theo's.

That evening brought a cooling breeze, a relief from the heat of the day; it dispersed the clouds to revel crystal clear stars. The insects intense chirping kept me awake, and reminded me of home and Africa. For once, I felt homesick and my family lay on my heart. I hope they are well.

A Letter from Ma

Three months after Christmas a letter arrived from ma. Sad news. Pa had passed away suddenly; he had suffered a stroke. I was heartbroken, as I was so far away from the family. Pa had worked hard all his life, to provide a better life for his family. Ma writes that he was buried in the local church and that the ceremony and wake were well attended. Pa was known and liked by many people. Ma writes that she is bearing up, taking it easy, but has moved in with Jacob and his family. Jacob has now taken over the blacksmith forge. Jacob's wife, Amelia was the daughter of the local general store in Greytown. Their daughter Catherine and son Jude were both well.

There was further news about the family. Annie, my sister, her husband August and daughter Minnie had now moved to Durban. August worked in the newspaper print industry and there was more opportunity of work there. Thomas my second brother was doing well in the Church and was now vicar in Ladysmith. My youngest brother, who was a teacher, had finally got engaged to Charlotte, who was also a teacher. So, some good news to end a sad letter.

Dreamtime

A kookaburra calls,
To wake me from my midnight slumber.
A hot clammy breeze blows through.
The light voile curtains across my face.
A golden orb spins and retracts,
To the safety of its silky latticework.
A rumble of thunder and a crack of lightning,
Splinters the deep blackness of the purple night sky.

Echoes of canyons, primitive boulders and painted caves.

Summon up the sound of the didgeridoo and a spirit of
dreamtime walkers.
I turn to lucid sleepy dreams,
Of pathways through thickened heated rainforest roots.
Lush and wet the rain falls,
Creating a shiny reflective viscous coating on large green
leaved plants.

As the sweet warm rain cascades hitting the balcony roof,
It bounces off the canvas to land on unsuspecting croaking
blue frogs below.
The water collects in vats of treacly liquid,
A liquor of rotting smells that attracts unsuspecting creatures
to drop.

While wild orchids cling to vines of deep-rooted trees,
And brings a light to the night of the forest.
An iguana approaches, sniffing tongue on air,
He turns with a flick of his tail to an undergrowth of leaves.
The Daintree stretches before me winding and curling,
Hugging the banks of the forest as it goes.

The scent of dry crisp euphoric red eucalyptus trees,
Tease and tantalise my senses.
A ghostly white gum tree, inhabited by the spirits of the
dead,
Shines brightly, as it peers from behind flashes of colour,
Of golden bouquets to scarlet bottlebrush trees.
While Fairy wrens emerge from tangled wiry stems hung,
from forest creepers
To watch lorikeets feed tipsily on sweet nectareous blossom.

Turtles pop their heads above to catch lone dragonflies
Despite larger ancient dragons watching from banks whilst
dozing.
The river finally flows to the buzzing popping mangroved
flats,
Out beyond, to a sea of deep magical coral delights.
Where once the Yirrganydji people walked,
Along the limestone cliffs, now submerged.
By the deep blue ocean.

Dreamtime or Dreaming

*English can never capture what 'Dreaming' or
'Dreamtime' is all about. The Dreaming is linked to the
creation process and spiritual ancestors, and is still around
today. Aboriginal spirituality does not consider the
'Dreamtime' as a time past, in fact not as a time at all. Time
refers to past, present and future but the 'Dreamtime' is none
of these. The 'Dreamtime' "is there with them, it is not a long
way away. The Dreamtime is the environment that the
Aboriginal lived in and it still exists today, all around us." It
is important to note that the Dreaming always also comprises
the significance of place. Hence, if we try to use an English
word, we should avoid the term 'Dreamtime' and use the
word 'Dreaming' instead. It expresses better the timeless
concept of moving from 'dream' to reality which in itself is an
act of creation and the basis of many Aboriginal creation
myths. None of the hundreds of Aboriginal languages contain
a word for time.*

*The Dreaming also explains the creation process.
Ancestor beings rose and roamed the initially barren land,*

fought and loved, and created the land's features as we see them today. After creating the 'sacred world' the spiritual beings "turned into rocks or trees or a part of the landscape. These became sacred places, to be seen only by initiated men." The spirits of the ancestor beings are passed on to their descendants, e.g., shark, kangaroo, honey ant, snake and so on and hundreds of others which have become totems within the diverse Indigenous groups across the continent Each Aboriginal person identifies with a specific Dreaming. It gives them identity, dictates how they express their spirituality and tells them which other Aboriginal people are related to them in a close family, because those share the same Dreaming. One person can have multiple Dreamings Each form shares the spirituality from the 'Dreaming'. It is during ceremonies that the trance-like dreaming state seizes the Aboriginal people and they connect with the ancestral beings. http://www.creativespirits.info/aboriginalculture/spirituality/ what-is-the-dreamtime-or-the-dreaming#ixzz3arbxbmq7

Chapter Seven, Part Two:
The Great Black Swan

(A Dreamtime Creation Story)

During a family holiday to Australia Seren visited the Currumbin Wildlife Sanctuary on the Gold Coast of Australia. A group of Aboriginal dancers greeted the family. They lead them to a sandy area, surrounded by blue eucalyptus trees. They sat and watched, while the group played didgeridoos and danced to the earthly hollow sound. The eerie rhythmic music echoed and vibrated through the sand into Seren's very being. They asked the audience for volunteers, to get up and join them in their dance, Dad was encouraged to do so, how embarrassing! Each dancer was uniquely marked with exquisite embellishments. The coloured dots surrounded by bright whiteness seemed to move independently on the painted dancers' bodies. They had many meanings about their creation, ancestors, laws, religious beliefs and way of life; symbols of the Dreamtime which they told us about through their music, dance and song. The Aboriginal people, never wrote anything down, so their stories would be passed down to them from to generation to generation by these methods.

After Seren asked her dad to tell her a story about their creation, this is what he made up, about The Great Black Swan. One of the many native Australian animals.

"The Great Black Swan flew north. He flew on the breeze without stopping so eager was his journey. His wingspan was so vast that it caused a mighty shadow to fall across the land. The landscape red, dusty featureless a desolate plain with no animals or plants. After flying for many days, he saw what he was searching for. Her contrast to the landscape was astounding; she had been waiting for a long time. She was perched high on an outcrop, when she opened up her wings as the Black Swan approached, she was so pleased to see her partner and gave a loud honk to greet him. The beautiful female had been sat proudly, nurturing their magnificent egg. They greeted each other and spent time pruning each other's feathers and waiting for life to return. Days later the egg split in two and creation had begun. The top half of the egg formed the great escarpments, mountains, and canyons. The lower half of the egg formed the deep blue sky. The bluish liquid formed the rivers, lakes and coral seas. The yolk floated to the sky and became the great burning sun. The white of the inside

149

of the shell became the silvery moon and heavens. Colourful particles of shell formed the stars to light the night sky. Then the land shook and from the centre of the earth came the great dreamtime snake, emu and wallaby followed by the birds of the sky and the fish of the sea and rivers. Leaving behind Uluru. Life had returned and began anew. The Great Black Swan and his mate had fulfilled their purpose, and wondered at the awe they had created."

The Uluragoo

After the story Seren and her family walked around the rest of the sanctuary where they saw many different animals like koalas, kangaroos, emus, dingoes, wombats, Tasmanian devils and the colourful rainbow lorikeets. After that, they caught the bus back to their hotel.

That night Seren had a dream about the Dreamtime animals Koala, Snake, Emu, and Kangaroo.

In her dream, Seren was walking along a ridge in the Blue Mountains; she stopped to drink from a waterfall. The blue mist, (created from the oils in the eucalyptus leaves) that had surrounded her, started to clear and she came across a cave. On the cave, walls were ancient paintings, done a long time ago by the local people. The sea and the red land were painted with the sun above. In the painting were many of the animals Seren had seen in the park earlier that day. There was a kangaroo, emu, koala and even a snake. She sat down in the cool to enjoy the painting. Then it looked like the painting started to move, was it the heat creating a mirage? No, she looked again and it was beginning to come to life. It looked as if the kangaroo was calling to her. She got up and walked closer to the cave wall. The kangaroo reached out his paw to Seren, she grabbed it and the kangaroo began pulling her into the painting. Next thing she knew she was standing next to the kangaroo. Seren looked different, as if she had been painted. They greeted each other.

The animals seemed to be in a bit of disagreement. Seren asked Kangaroo what the problem was. Kangaroo said it was the Uluragoo that was causing the problems. Seren looked a bit surprised and asked what an Uluragoo was. Kangaroo said it was a very strange creature to describe as nobody had ever really seen one, it was a mythical creature but they knew it had an earthly form. "It normally lives at the centre of our land at Uluru; it has never been known to appear this far east in the Blue Mountains. We are very worried it wants to settle here because it is a bad omen and whenever it appears everything seems to dry up and die and we don't want that to happen here."

"What will you do?" asked Seren.

"We will have to come up with a plan, but we may need your help as with your red hair you have magical powers." Seren look a bit surprised as she was not aware, she had any magic.

Just then, the sky started to turn grey and the wind got up blowing the red dusty ground into their eyes. The leaves from the crisp eucalyptus trees started whirling around, dry lightning cracked in the distance creating the sound of a didgeridoo. The animals became very unsettled and afraid and did not know what to do. The ground began to shake and the noise became more intense. Through the dust they thought they could see a strange object, but it had no real form, it looked like a violent sun set full of flames and intense heat. As it got closer it began to take more shape, it was like nothing Seren had ever seen before. Yes, it had arms and legs, but its feet were webbed and hands were claws with one long protruding finger. Its main body was furry but had slimy red and orange scales on its chest. A head full of feathers for hair, with large scales running down its back that dispersed into a crocodilian tail that coiled behind it. Its eyes were the deepest shade of black and looked menacing. As it saw Seren, it was a bit hesitant in getting closer but it persevered.

Just as the creature was about to move within touching distance a flock of lorikeets came screeching out of the forest. A man, playing a didgeridoo followed them, he was a magic man. His skin was the colour of the burnt soil his white hair-tinged flame red as if it were on fire. When the creature saw him, it fled.

"Can you help us to keep the creature away?" Kangaroo asked the man.

"Yes, but I can only keep it away for a short time. I will need the help of the little girl to send it back to where it came from. But first I will need to let her dream to find the magic words to cast it out," he replied. He played his wooden instrument as Seren fell into dreamtime.

'Seren had been wandering the forest in her dream. The Uluragoo had been following her. She needed to reach safety. The high rock lands were her best bet, where Wombat lived. Here she would find safety and protection.

As she got closer to the hills, the terrain got harder to climb. She could see safety in the distance. Just then, she became frozen to the spot. She called to Mother Creation for protection.

Through the trees, she caught glimpses of the approaching Uluragoo. Time seemed to slow and she was pulled further back from the safety of her sanctuary. She could feel the Uluragoo breathing down her neck he was just about to reach out and grab her. Then Mother Creation swept her up under her cloak and carried her to the safety of the rocks where Wombat was waiting. There she rested.

"Please can you help me defeat the Uluragoo by giving me magic words to send him back from where he belongs?" Seren asked.

Wombat and Mother Creation spoke for a while and agreed to give her the magic words.

"These are the words you must say," they said together.

"Mystical being you cannot come to our land, you must depart, be gone back to where you came from and never come back."

"Say these words while the Magic Man is playing the didgeridoo."

Then the figures and their surroundings slowly disappeared as the dream ended.'

As Seren was stirring from the dream she woke saying, "I know how to defeat the Uluragoo. Mother Creation and Wombat have given me magic words to say that will send the Uluragoo back to where it comes from. As I cast the spell the Magic Man will play the didgeridoo."

They waited until the creature approached again. The lorikeets were circling above and the man was chanting away, sat cross-legged on the ground next to Seren who was standing on a rock. The wind picked up and was howling like last time. Seren's hair was wild and made her look mad in the wind. The man blew into the instrument and Seren started repeating the words Mother Creation and Wombat had told her, over and over again. The animals closed their eyes, as they could not bear to look.

"Mystical being you cannot come to our land, you must depart, be gone back to where you came from and never come back."

The creature kept moving closer and closer until he got sight of Seren, this time he froze to the spot and could not move.

"Louder, louder," said the Magic Man, "it's working."

"Mystical being, you cannot come to our land, you must depart, be gone back to where you came from and never come back."

The man blew louder and longer into the instrument and Seren shouted the words. "Mystical being you cannot come to our land, you must depart, be gone back to where you came from and never come back."

The creature gave one last growl, his look turned from menacing to fear. And with a final blow on the instrument, he disappeared into a million particles was got blown away by the wind. The animals were all so relieved and happy that when they opened their eyes and looked, they saw the man and the birds dancing for joy. Seren was still standing on the rock with the instrument to her lips.

"Ah all good, I will call you Gugarra Mirii (Red Star) as your magic is powerful," said the old man. "If you ever need me again, just dance and play music around a fire and I will return." He wondered off into the bush waving his goodbyes and the lorikeets followed.

It was time for Seren to go as well. The animals thanked her for her help and asked her to come back anytime as she stepped out of the painting. She was back in the cave in the Blue Mountains. The sound of the wind blew through the cave Ser, Ser, Ser. It was magical but haunting.

"Seren, Seren wake up it's time for breakfast," Mum called.

Time for another adventure Seren thought.

The Great Cassowary

Seren's family were travelling north by train to visit Kuranda. They entered the carriages and sat on the long seats with its soft cracked brown leather, our bags safely stored on racks above. Seren pulled the windows down to let the air circulate. The journey took us up and out of Cairns through lowland farms and tea plantations. On through lush ancient rainforest. The train wound its way through tunnels, over sturdy metal bridges, deep ravines and passing cascading waterfalls. Their final destination a colonial train station in the heart of the rainforest with its red metal roof and hanging orchid baskets. Their hotel 'Gone Walkabout'.

After a busy train journey, we all went for an afternoon nap. Seren dreamt of her dreamtime friends.

When she arrived, there was great commotion. Something was not right. She could not see Emu or Koala, but Snake and Kangaroo were there.

"Oh, Seren we are so pleased to see you, something terrible had happened. Emu and Koala had gone walkabout when there was a great dust storm appeared from nowhere and when it cleared, they were gone," said Kangaroo.

"We sent Cockatoo to fly around to see if she could find them, but there was no sign," said Snake.

There had been talk in the north of the return of the Great Cassowary, a very evil bird. Could there be a link?

"We must call upon the Magic Man to help us to find out what has happened to them," said Seren.

So that night they called upon him with dancing and music around the camp fire. As a puff of smoke rose from the fire the man appeared before them form out of the rock as if he had always been there.

"You have returned oh great and wonderful Red Star 'Gugarra Mirii'," said the man.

"Yes, I felt that my friends were in distress and needed help." Seren then explained to him what had happened to Emu and Koala.

They all sat around the fire, the man crossed legged next to Seren. He took some orange dust out of a small brown leather pouch attached to a rope around his waist, which he threw into the fire, as he muttered some words, bright orange sparks flew out of the crackling spitting flames. He then went into a trance swaying from side to side, and then he stopped and stared into the fire, still chanting. The smoke began to clear and there above was an image of Emu and Koala, they were calling for help. They had got lost and confused when the dust storm arrived and ended up walking in the wrong direction. When the dust storm cleared, they found themselves in a strange place.

There was a noise behind them and when they turned to look, there had been a pack of Tasmanian devils following them. They were afraid and tried to run and hide, but the devils captured them. They took them to the Cassowary, who then imprisoned them. Seren and her friends could see them trapped in a cave feeling sad and afraid to be away from their friends. The image then cleared and at that point, the Magic Man came out of his trance.

"How can we help them?" Seren exclaimed sorrowfully. "Will you come with us too?" she asked the man.

"Yes," he replied, "we must come up with a plan as the Great Cassowary is a very powerful and dangerous creature with many spies and helpers. His pride is expressed through its velvety, deep, rich plumage. He will overpower all the land, its people and animals, we must stop him," the Magic Man was very serious in his reply.

They came up with a plan that would save Emu and Koala and trap the Cassowary in a dream spell.

"We must appeal to his pride," said the man.

This is what happened.

So, they disguised themselves as the most colourful animals you would ever see, they looked like a carnival, a palette of feathers, flowers, leaves, branches and colourful dyes made from the soil of the earth. They were a sight to be seen as they marched across the desert to find their friends. There was Dingo, Snake, Kangaroo, Seren and the Magic Man and all the other animals and birds playing musical instruments as they marched.

Off they went following the footsteps of Emu and Koala, until they saw a dust storm approaching, they took cover, and when the storm had cleared and ended up in a strange place they did not know. They travelled carefully as they knew Cassowary would have his spies out looking.

They came across the Tasmanian devils who were taken aback and surprised by the sight they were looking at. So quickly, the Magic Man cast a spell on them that put them in a trance and under his control. This would allow them to approach the place where the Great Cassowary lived. This was on a high stony outcrop, surrounded by a forest; there was only one way in and one way out. The cave that Emu and Koala were trapped in was beneath the stony outcrop.

Seren found a way in to see if they were OK, and even though they were exhausted and hungry, they were really pleased to see her. She told them of their plan to rescue them.

The next day Cassowary was looking proudly at his Kingdom when he saw the strange colourful party, he was intrigued by their flamboyancy, and decided to trick them into his camp. There he would kill them and take all their amazing beauty and colour. For it would not do that there was something more colourful than him, his pride would not allow it. Little did he know but this was part of the group's plan, for once, they were in his camp they could set to work. So, he approached the group of travellers with niceties. The group pretended to not know who he was; they accepted his initiation into his camp.

That evening they went to dine with Cassowary around his fire. The Cassowary thought he had the better of these unsuspecting fools as he had cast a spell over the food. However, little did he know that the group had a spell of their own to cast. Therefore, instead of eating the food first they said they would dance and sing around the fire for him, to say thank you for inviting them in. As they were singing and dancing Cassowary thought, they were too happy and was getting irritable but their spell was being cast as they sang and danced before him. A dream spell was spun over the fire.

"Our dream is cast into the fire,

The magic woven from our wishes,

Spun into the stars of time,

Fallen from the night sky to embers below,

But now the suns rising is almost upon us,

Our dream time deed is done before we leave and go away."

He was trapped in the devil's fire he could not do anything, his powers were useless, the spell was too strong, there was too many of them. As the dream spell opened up it dragged Cassowary into a faraway place, it then closed behind him, never to re-open.

After this, the Tasmanian devils awoke from their trance and they were set free, because Cassowary had tricked them too. The group then went to release Emu and Koala. They were so happy to be reunited with their friends. The Magic Man helped them to return home.

As they said their goodbyes, the group told Seren that she must come back in happier times.

Seren then woke from her afternoon nap, called her mum and dad and they went to explore the colourful town of Kuranda its markets and all the wonders it had to offer.

The next day they ventured further into the Australian rainforest and to Cape Tribulation, what dreams Seren would have there?

NEW ZEALAND

Chapter Eight, Part One: Aotearoa – The Land of the Long White Cloud

New Zealand, 1885–1888

About six months ago, Theo was introduced to a man called James Hector who was the manager of the Botanical Gardens in Wellington New Zealand. He had been visiting Australia gathering plants for the garden. After he realised Theo's background, he offered him a job as his deputy. Theo fell in love with the idea of returning to his fist passion. The banana plantation had been doing well, but it was time to move on. We booked passage on the SS Rotorua a passenger ship sailing regularly from Cairns to Wellington. Litiana decided to come with us as well. So, we upsticks again. We have now been here for two months and have settled in an area close to the gardens called Kelburn, with impressive views over Wellington harbour. With the help of Litiana, I was able to re-establish the Lavender farm with cuttings that I brought with us. The climate here in New Zealand was perfect for the lavender, which thrived.

1886

The farm is looking particularly lovely this year; the crop yield will be good. We should have enough flowers to dry this year to make fragrant linen sachets for linen closets and wardrobes. Apart from that, we will make lavender oil to soothe headaches and it can be used for an antiseptic and to calm insect bites. The dark honey is sticky and delicious. However, my favourite is making the soap bars. Lavender has so many special properties and you can do many wonderful things with it.

1888

After several years had passed Theo and I felt it was time to return to England. There were several reasons; one was due to the many earthquakes in the area plus the recent eruption of Mount Tarawera. This disaster had buried many nearby Maori settlements and caused loss of life. We felt unsettled in the area. Recently, Theo had spoken to a British businessman, who was watching a rugby match, (the first Tour of the British Lions to New Zealand) he told him how prosperous England was, once again. Theo wanted to establish his own mini-Kew Gardens back in England and I longed for the adventures I had as a child in Devon.

A Last Adventure: Summer 1889

Not long before we were due to leave, we had heard of an American aerialist called Professor Baldwin who was touring the country. Performing from his tethered balloon his shows had a reputation of great excitement. As the balloon would rise a trapeze artist would perform and at the end the Professor would jump from the balloon attached to a parachute.

A show we had to see, one which lived up to all expectations.

People gathered, with an air of anticipation, on an open space at the Botanical gardens, normally where the local county fayre was held. Around the outside there was a big wheel, small side shows and stall holders selling local produce. With the balloon taking centre stage, towering over us all. The scene was set.

The Professor and his trapeze artist came out from a tent nearby. Dressed like a circus master, and in a big booming voice, welcomed us all, and explained we were to see an act never seen before. They climbed into the bright yellow balloon, as soon as it was set off, the trapeze artist climbed the ropes and swung from side to side. The higher and higher it got the more extreme her leaps of elegance seemed to get and the more dangerous. There were gasps from the crowd as our hearts beat faster and faster and great cheers of relief as she landed safely back in the balloon. As the act came to a close one more defying feat as the Professor just launched himself from the balloon. Falling, falling the crowd held their breath and looked on in amazement. Then his parachute opened full of colour and glory as he glided to the ground, to an almighty roar of cheers, hoorays and claps raised by his appreciative captivated audience. Myself I wondered how wonderful it would be to go up in the balloon.

So, at the end of the day when most folk had left, we approached the Professor and asked if he would like to come and stay a while, in return for a flight in his balloon. He agreed.

The very next day Theo and I set off with the Professor on a breath-taking journey over this wilderness of great beauty with dramatic landscapes. We floated above mountain peaks, with sulphuric volcano peaks, where the air was cold and thin. Through high sided winding valleys, with fast flowing milky rivers below. Below us, dense native forest spread out for miles and miles. Eerie places where the mist hung low, occasionally viewing strange giant like shapes formed by this ever-changing, moving land or by the Gods of old. The journey, reminded me of when I was a child as the wind picked up and whipped my hair over my face. The feelings I had, as I looked out over the harbour in Plymouth and to the Eclipse, of freedom and the anticipation of a new life in a strange land, all came flooding back to me. England was now that strange land.

After our spectacular journey, I expressed in a poem, Aotearoa – The Land of the Long White Cloud. The Professor stayed with us for a few nights and then travelled onto his next show.

The Journey Home

The journey would be long, a sea crossing with the Oceanic Steamship Co to San Francisco with a stop in Hawaii. Then a railway crossing across America. Finally, back to sea, from New York to Liverpool, on the SS City of New York.

Litiana was now married and with her first child on the way, New Zealand had now become her home. I left the farm to her as she had spent so much time with me establishing it, making, and selling the products.

We gave ourselves plenty of time to organise the crossing, packing our belongings and sending them on ahead. As well as contacting family back in England to let them know, we would be returning home.

Finally, another last day arrived and brought tears of sadness at leaving our friends behind, especially Litiana, who was more like a member of our family. We hugged her so tightly to create one lasting memory, and said our farewells.

Aotearoa – The Land of the Long White Cloud

Lost in a blanket of soft white curling clouds,
Emerging above prehistoric hanging valleys and hidden waterfalls,
Rising up, up, up on a cool draft of air,

Far above mountains capped with ice crystals
Where the snow maiden Hukatere has spread her cloak for winter.
Upward over glistening blue white glacier pinnacles,
While down below run deep gravelly winding milky cream and jade wild rivers,
Hineteiwaiwa the moon Goddess lights our way,
Over pancake rocks where midnight rainbows appear in the sea spray,
Onward through narrow waterways saturated by overhanging ferns and nikaus, no time to rest.
Glass like clarity of the dawn maidens light arrives and greets us,
While the silent misty Goddesses' fingers descend from the mountains,
Where, beneath a canopy of silver and green punga,
She meets her love Tane, God of dense gully tree ferns in an eternal blending of magic and myth,
The Tui and Kereru join in our mystical flight with their morning songs.
Golden sands caress sheltered coves,
With hidden caves and rocks of old dotted with lush dense forest,
Rivers cascade to estuaries below, twisting roots line winding pathways.
Then silent grey bodies arise from the Orangorango,
Where the spirits of the dead now roam.
Beyond the scorched desert road to the charcoaled escarpments,
Where giants roamed and laid down to sleep,
We soar as the smokey heat rises from below,

The God of volcanoes Ruaumoko erupts to glorious cause,
Spilling his golden sulphuric guts to plunder the vast green
spaces.
The Poi* speaks to me, its percussive voice is carried on the
winds,
Its dance lives in the waves on the sea, soft like the snow
falling from the clouds,
Its creator Tānemahuta, the ancestral God of the forests is
pleased.
In contrast creeks of lavender deeply scented, strong and
pungent,
A field of blue, a place to drift, the soft buzz, sanctuary for
the honeybee.
We drift further north to our final resting place,
The fiery red flamed pōhutukawa trees below guide the way,
To blackened mirrored lakes and cliffed coves of golden
sands,
Where earthy smells blend with the sweet-scented blossom
of the kowhai tree floating dreamily on high,
Aroah** for the land of the long white cloud.

*Poi refers to both a style of performing and the
equipment used for engaging in poi performance. Wikipedia.
**Maori for love.

Chapter Eight, Part Two:
The Orange Tree

Whilst in New Zealand, Seren and her family would spend many Sunday afternoons exploring Wilton Bush a small native garden area on the edge of Wellington, New Zealand. There they would picnic and paddled in the streams under the dappled sunlight. Go on walks, over fern covered bridges and try to spot the magical, sacred kingfisher or fairy martin birds. They would also make up adventures and tell made stories of the mythical folk that once lived in New Zealand. Here is one such tale, set nearby.

The tale of the Orange Tree grew deep within the mystical native forests on New Zealand's North Island, between Taupo and Napier. You would only find it if you were not seeking it. It was told to have magical healing powers and its secret was hidden deep within Maori folk law. Nobody knew exactly where it was, it would just appear and disappear when needed. The Patu Paiarehe, the faerie people of this entrancing land, protected the tree.

Seren had been playing with her friends in the park behind the house, back in Devon. It was a hot sunny day and Seren felt like a rest. She sat on the swing seat underneath the walnut tree at the top of the garden. A blackbird sung his summer song while Seren drifted into sleep, as the chair dreamily swayed back and forth.

Seren woke to an eerie silence that was soon broken by the echoing sound of a tui*. Calling, through the dense mist, which surrounded her, from high above in a kauri tree. She did not recognise the bird song, or where she was. The surroundings had changed, but she felt safe. The mist quickly lifted as the shimmering sun's rays begun to break through.

Now she was fully awake Seren could see the tree had changed into a punga tree, its soft curly leaves creating an enchanting lattice pattern on her face and arms. It created the look of her being tattooed. As she got up to walk away to her surprise her imaginary kirituhi** stayed with her.

Seren walked for a while through the native bush followed by fantails** picking off little bugs as she kicked them up with her feet. The bush was now becoming denser so it was a challenge to get through, she was lost. However, up ahead she could see an orange glow, which was comforting; by now, she was beginning to feel hungry. As she got closer and closer to the glow, the dense forest opened up into a clearing with the most vibrant of orange trees she had ever seen. She did not expect to see such a tree here. The tree was unusually full with fragranced blossom due to the branches being laden with the largest oranges Seren had ever seen. The tree swayed in the gentle breeze the warm sun shining down creating a winsome atmosphere. An orange, fell from a branch, Seren took this as a sign, that the tree wanted her to eat. She picked it up and started to peel the orange, it was so juicy, the flesh blood orange. She broke it into segments, its nectar so sweet, the segments, so nourishing, that when she had finished eating, she felt satisfied. Seren sat down for a rest and began wondering how to get out of the forest.

"Can you help me to find my way out of the forest?" Seren asked the tree.

The wind whistled through the tree and Seren understood her reply. "I can, but I will summon the faeries of the forest to help you." The tree called for the faeries as her orange blossom drifted through the air.

From under the surrounding flowers appeared the most delicate of creatures with tiny fluorescent wings. At first, Seren thought they looked like butterflies, but then she could see they had tiny human like faces, and wore clothes shaped from flowers and leaves.

"We are the Patu Paiarehe the faerie folk who live here and protect the tree."

"We will help you, find you way out," said the faeries.

Seren was very grateful to the tree for her help and the orange. As she left, she made a blessing to the tree that her spirit would continue to shine a light through the forest. The faeries led Seren back, out of the glade, through the forest back to the tree where she started her journey. The tui was still singing above. While Seren sat down the faeries asked her if they could tell her a story about the Princess Tawera.

Princess Tawera

Once long ago in the ancient Kauri Forest lived an evil troll king who was an enemy to the Patu Paiarehe folk of the Punga Tree Valley. He wanted to capture the beautiful Princess Tawera (which means, Morning Star) with her red skin and golden tinged hair. He knew every evening she walked across a bridge of moss and fern, soft as silence barefoot she would go, to a magical place, where she would meet her love Prince Ihaia. She was to marry him, to make an alliance with the people of the Smokey Mountains, but the jealous troll king wanted her for himself.

'As she waited upon her love
Beneath a canopy of gold and green
A sprinkle of evening sunshine on dew drops glisten
Serenity and magic a pool awaits
A place to bathe and glow anew
She awaited her love
Under a river of stars
Alas this night, Ihaia never did arrive.'

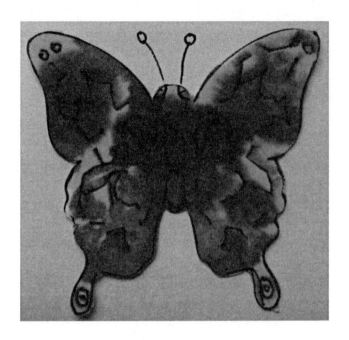

The troll king sent an evil faerie spirit Maero to capture the princess. Maero took a magic potion to transform himself into Prince Ihaia. He cast a spell, sending Tawera into a deep sleep; he then took her to the troll king.

Now the Patu Paiarehe are peaceful beings and King Turehu, Tawera's father, did not know what to do. He called upon his friends and allies the Turehu the pale-skinned ghostly spirits of the woodland realms to help him free his daughter. They sent many soldiers to claim her back, many died in the battle that followed. The troll king would not give up his prize easily. However, eventually they found her safe and well and returned her to her father. In return, Tuehu honoured the Turehu with special cloaks made out of rare yellow feathers, he was so grateful for their help.

Alas a few months later the Princess was re captured by the troll king. Tuehu was very worried and did not want to trouble his friends the Turehu again or tell Prince Ihaia of his troubles. One day while he was walking in his gardens, he met a cloaked woman, her name was Rehua. She asked why the King was so worried; he had nobody to talk to as his Queen had died many years ago, so he told her about his daughter. The woman thought for a moment and told the King that she could help him. Nevertheless, his daughter and the prince would have to live in her Kingdom after their third child was born. He agreed, as he would have done anything to save his daughter.

Rehua returned sometime later with his daughter, he was very happy. She must be very powerful he thought, so did not ask how she had saved her. No more was heard of from the troll king.

Later, the wedding between Tawera and Ihaia went ahead and all in their Kingdoms were happy. Now, after their third child had been born, Rehua returned as promised, in all her shinning glory, for her kingdom was Ika-Roa (Milky Way). Tuehu thought the day would never arrive, as they were all so happy. The King would have his three grandchildren but he would have to say goodbye to his daughter and son in law. He told them of the pact he had made with Rehua. Tears were shed. Rehua cast a spell and made the two into the brightest morning stars in the heavens. The King was very sad; his heart was broken at what he had done. He would never be able to hug his daughter again. Nevertheless, he would watch for her coming over the horizon in early morning sky. He would be reminded of her, knowing she was safe for eternity and his heart would be warmed.

Rehua then revealed her true self to the King. He had met her when he was young, before he met his wife; she was his first true love. However, his father did not allow their love. Turehu's father banished her to the starry kingdom. Now it was time for Rehua to return to this earthly realm and rekindle her love for Tuehu.

Later, when the King died, Rehua cast a spell over him to re-unite him and his daughter in the starry heavens.

The tale was told, which Seren enjoyed.

After the story, the faeries sprinkled some magic dust over Seren. They told her that she would fall to sleep and when she would wake up, she would be back under the tree she originally fell asleep under. As she fell to sleep, she whispered her goodbyes blessing the spirits of the forest, giving them thanks for looking after her.

A few moments later Seren awoke under the walnut tree and went to find her friends. "Did you miss me?" Seren asked them, as she felt like she'd been away for ages.

"You've only been gone a few minutes," they said. Seren turned back to see that the walnut tree had returned.

She looked at her arm and even though the patterns created by the sun's rays through the punga tree creating the kirituhi had gone, she was left with an image of a fantail that reminded her of her adventure and the faeries, a butterfly swooped past and off she went to play.

*a large New Zealand honeyeater bird with glossy blackish plumage and two white tufts at the throat.

**Kirituhi is a Māori style tattoo either made by a non-Māori tattooer, or made for a non-Māori wearer. Kirituhi has mana of its own and is a design telling the unique story of the wearer in the visual language of Māori art and design. Kiri means 'skin', and tuhi means 'to write, draw, record, adorn or decorate with painting' http://www.tarynberi.com

***The fantail is one of New Zealand's best-known birds, with its distinctive fanned tail and loud song, and particularly because it often approaches within a metre or two of people. Its wide distribution and habitat preferences, including frequenting well-treed urban parks and gardens, means that most people encounter fantails occasionally.

http://nzbirdsonline.org.nz

HAWAII

Chapter Nine, Part One: Aloha

Hawaii, 1889 – Stopover En-Route Home

A welcome break from the turbulent Pacific Ocean. A heavenly rest for the tourists at a turbulent time for the people of Hawaii. We were greeted at the port with garlands of flowers know as leis. Dancers and singers greeted us to their beguiling island. A stopover for a couple of days before continuing our journey to San Francisco.

Even though the people greeted us with happiness, there was sadness in their eyes. For after many years of prosperity, there was unrest in the country. The Kings' health was failing and there was pressure from the Unites States to annex the Kingdom of Hawaii. King Kalakaua was known as The Merrie Monarch, and the people loved him He with his sister Princess Lili'uokalani (who later became Queen), travelled to England, on a similar route to ours, a few years previous to attend Queen Victoria's Golden Jubilee. What a sight that must have been.

We arrived at a time when the Hula dance and Kapa* fabric making showed a revival. We came to understand the Hula was an expression of the heart and the very pulse of the Hawaiian people and Kapa created a strength of fortitude, unity and independence.

After refreshing ourselves at our hotel, we were taken to watch an evening show of a hula performed by a group of talented dancers. The hula was created to praise the Gods and Goddesses, this play was for the Goddess Pele. The mystical, epic tale of oral Hawaiian history was expressed through dance and Oli chants, where power comes from Mana, a spiritual source.

The story was told of the Goddesses Pele and one of her sisters Hi'iaka, and of how the first King of Hawaii was blessed by the Gods and presented with a cape made of yellow feathers for all the good deeds he had done for his people. A great honour, as these yellow birds were very rare, and the cape took many feathers to make. It told of Pele's visit to the land where she fell in love with the King. Her sister saw this and was jealous. She decided to steal the King's cape and blame Pele. The King was very distraught and would not see Pele who returned to the heavens. Hi'iaka returned the cape to the King thinking he would fall in love with her, but he did not for his heart was broken. Hi'iaka realised her mistake and threw herself into the biggest volcano on the island. Pele saw this and returned to the land and was reunited with the King.

The tale was told and no sooner than we had arrived on the island, the next day it was time to leave.

* Kapa is a fabric made by native Hawaiians from the fibres of certain species of trees and shrubs in the orders Rosales and Malvales.

Aloha

Timeless eternal islands borne of mist and dream
Where majestical waterfalls end in deep green fern draped
valleys.
Magical and mysterious the fiery mountain bleeds
To the black sands of endless shifting of boulders and
burning sea.
Oh, Islands that grew out of the sea by the hand of the Gods.
Vessel of steam are enchantingly drawn into harbour's bay
Where we are greeted with lei* upon lei of exotically
fragrant flowers.
Maile** for the men with its heady vines blessed by the
Goddess Laka.

Given freely with a kiss our Mana*** is absorbed by the gift
Never to be given away in a vial of sweet essence.
A barefoot tale to be told of an ancient culture.
We dance to the heartbeat of the Hawaiian people.
As arms, feet and hips act as poetry, our faces express the story.
The Mele**** is woven into the dance as we are invited to join.
So too is the kapa***** as we are enlightened to their layered complex society.
Oh, great Gods of the Pacific may these sweet islands be your home.
Kane, the Sun God preserver of life, father of Mahina Goddess of the Moon.
The fiery Goddess Pele, of thunderous mountains rest at the edge of Kanoloa.
Ku, fly away winged God of War to greet Kapo Goddess of the South.
Valley floor to mountain top Lilinoe Goddess of mist mingles with Poli'ahu the Snow Goddess.
Time approaches to leave the Isles of isolated beauty and enigma.
Flowers of farewell and good luck are dispersed amongst the waves.
Into the sea as our vessel departs the water rich in abundant life.
Whales gather and sing their song of sadness drifting from these Hawaiian shores.
As a last look, mist and smoke combine high above Kilauea and Mauna Loa.

*Lei: Polynesian garland of flowers.

**Maile: vined lei for men.

***Mana: an impersonal supernatural power which can be transmitted or inherited.

****Mele: are chants, songs, or poems. The term comes from the Hawaiian language.

*****Kappa: is a fabric made by Native Hawaiians from the base fibres of certain species of trees and shrubs in the orders Rosales and Malvales. Kappa depended on caste and a person's place in ancient Hawaiian society.

Chapter Nine, Part Two: Hina and Her Sons

Seren has spent all afternoon practicing the new dances for the pantomime. This year it was Treasure Island and for one of the dances she had to dress up as a girl from a pacific island with a grass skirt and leis made of flowers. She remembered Bess has spent some time in Hawaii, on her way home, and went to find her journal. She wanted to see if Bess had done any writing, sketches or paintings while she was there to inspire her with her dance. There she found sketches of girls dancing the hula and pressed flowers form a lei. Tired after all her dancing and research Seren fell asleep.

She found herself dreaming of Pacific Gods and sacred islands. Here is her dream.

Hina, the mother, had three sons Hema, Puna and Maui. They were all very handsome and strong and Hina was very proud of them.

As they were growing up, she was very protective of them and hid them in a cave behind the Rainbow Falls on a small Pacific Island. She kept them from danger, especially Pele, her sister the Goddess of Volcanoes. She was very jealous of them, and the love Hina had for her husband Ku the feathered God of War, as Pele wanted Ku for herself.

Hina knew she would not be able to hide them in the cave forever. Pele would eventually find them and try to kill them with her fiery temper.

Hina had to work out ways to keep her sons safe and out of Pele's harm.

Firstly, she went to speak to Kanoloa, the God of the Oceans to see if he could help. He said he would but first Hema would have to do something in return for keeping him safe.

He would have to travel to a faraway place to kill a sea dragon that was endangering his seafaring people. However, on the way he was captured by Aiaia (a bird, messenger of the God Kane), who thought he was an enemy of Kanoloa. Hema called to his brothers through a giant conk shell to come and rescue him. They heard his call and came to his aid. As tricksters they then defeated the sea dragon, by disguising themselves with spiny scales from the fire sea urchin. They were able to get close to the sea dragon and overpower it with the poisonous spines.

Hina went back to Kanoloa to tell him the good news, but she was not sure that he could be trusted to keep his word; the God of the sea could be unpredictable. However, he was very grateful for the help and said in return that Hema could marry his daughter but to do so he would have to become a Merman and live in the deep oceans but he would always be safe under his protection. His transformation begun, as he dived into the sea the moonlight illuminated him. Kanoloa cast a spell upon him that transformed his legs into a tail with a flipper at the end, his scales glistened purple, green and gold in the fluorescent light. He liked his new body as he pirouetted in the sky splashing back to swim amongst the coral and fish.

His wife was a beautiful mermaid called Polina Oona and they lived very happily together. They swam far out to the Pacific atolls far away from man and where Pele would never search. They lived in the deepest part of the bluest Ocean.

Hina was pleased he was safe. But now for Maui and Puna.

Secondly, Hina approached Kane the Sun God to help her with her second son Maui. He too had a task for Maui before he would protect him.

The sky was falling on the people of the land making them suffer and not go about their lives. Kane wanted Maui, who was strong and muscular, to hold up the sky to allow the people to live and so he as the Sun God could shine down on them. Maui was doing well until the earth shook and Pele started getting angry. Maui called for his brother to help him keep the sky up. Puna came to help him and together by planting large hairy seeds they found floating in the sea. They grew into the life-giving coconut trees that were able to separate the earth from the sky to stop it from falling down.

Kane was very happy with Maui as he could see the people were happy and could go about their business. So, he decided to keep him safe from Pele by allowing him to move freely from the land as a man and the sky as a spirit in times of danger. He became a shape shifter. He married Lilinoe the Goddess of Mist, and they would meet together in spirit form when Lilinoe descended from the mountain tops and Maui would transform from a man to spirit as he rose into the sky, they would meet in the forests around the mountains.

Now Hina only had one son left Puna to find a safe place for. So Hina approached Poli'ahu the snow Goddess, who was the sister and rival to Pele. Hina knew that this would anger Pele very much so she had to be very careful.

She asked Poli`ahu if she would help keep her son safe from Pele. Poli`ahu agreed but in return Hina would have to do something for her. Poli`ahu had a cape made of white feathers that she wore in the winter to cover the mountain but in the summer, she wanted a cape made of silver from the beams of the moon. As Hina had a relationship with the moon she was able to capture the beams and spin the finest luxuriant cloth that she then wove into a cloak. When she presented the cape to Poli`ahu she was overwhelmed.

Pele discovered what Hina had done for Poli`ahu and she was very angry that she erupted causing the earth to burn with lava. Puna was not yet safe, so Poli`ahu shed her white cloak over the land to put Pele's fire out.

She was then able to help Hina and keep Puna safe. She sent him to a distant island that had no volcanoes on but many caves where he was able to live happily and surf in the waves around the island which was his favourite pastime. He changed his name to Wakea. He married the Goddess Kapo of the South Pacific. They became the parents of the ruling High Chiefs of the Pacific Islands.

Pele was so angry with Hina because she had been tricked. She then searched and searched for the brothers, but they could not be found anywhere. Nobody knew of their whereabouts, so in her anger she erupted like she never had done so before. She formed so many new volcanoes that she created the series of islands now called Hawaii.

Hina feeling unsafe for herself went back to the cave, hidden by the waterfall and waited for a new rainbow to arrive. At which point she climbed onto it; the rainbow took her to the moon. Where she became known as Mahina Goddess of the moon, and from where she could look down upon her sons and know they were safe.

Seren woke from her dream and told us her story. She then went back to practice her dance moves ready for the pantomime, which she got to perform on stage later that year.

AMERICA

Chapter Ten, Part One:
Across the Rocky Road

America, 1889

We arrived in the Port of San Francisco after our long voyage and enjoyable stopover in Hawaii. The city was called the Paris of the West; its architecture certainly lived up to that. Set on an endless hill, the city boasted some wonderful houses. We stayed in a borders house for a few days in readiness for our journey across America on the Transatlantic Train. As tourists, we spent a day in the city. At the Golden Gate Park, with its views of the hidden harbour and displaced totem poles. Travelling on the newly constructed cable car, to the wharf. In the heat of the day, we stopped to rest at a mission station where we watched humming birds gather nectar from exotic flowers.

We arrived at the train station in plenty of time. A large station with several platforms, all with trains, waiting to be bordered. Our departure was to begin from platform three, on our epic journey across this land. The platform was a bustle with passengers, porters, trunks and suitcases. Our porter greeted us, took our trunks, and loaded them onto the train. He then showed us to our carriage.

It was small but comfortable, and a bit of a squeeze as the journey would take us three days. At least there were pull down beds we could sleep in at night. There was also a small washroom attached to the compartment too.

Our journey got underway through the flatlands that surrounded the city, out into farmland, mainly of corn and wheat, and some with vast herds of cattle. The farms were enormous here compared to New Zealand; farmhouses surrounded by trees for shade to protect them against the Californian sunshine. The scenery begun to change, as we left the homesteads, to meadows full of red poppies and bright yellow star shaped flowers. Then we started to climb to forests and lakes. Endless rows of sycamore, aspen and cottonwood trees. Followed by fir and pine trees.

Gorges cut through valleys of giant sequoia and redwoods as the train continues to wind its way up the foothills of the Great Rockies. Through endless tunnels, twisting, winding following rivers along ravines over bridges spanning wide gorges, with white water flowing below. Eventually we arrived at the top of the continental divide; snow lay on the ground it was still only spring. The train came to a holt and we were able to get out and stretch our legs. The bright bluish sunshine was still cold. Cute inquisitive chipmunks came to visit, eager for scraps of food.

The journey down the other side was of equal dramatic scenery with cascading tumbling waterfalls, with sheer cliff faces, leading to the majestic prairies ahead.

The heat begun building as the train journeyed further into the vast grasslands dotted with vibrant blue cornflowers. The carriage became overwhelmingly stuffy; I drifted off to sleep to the rattling chug, chug, puff, puff sound of the train.

I was woken by the sound of crows cawing to one another as they circled the train. I got up to open the window, the smell of perfumed lotus and wild geranium filled the carriage. Smoke drifted over the distant horizon. The noisy crows left leaving the sound of the breeze whispering to me through the tall grasses. The smoke, now bewitching, lifts, as a woman emerges holding a large shell. She is the Great Clan Mother. An evocative sound evaporates into the air and she blows into the shell. She calls forth the Ancestral Spirits of her people to hunt on the plains for the last time. First, the buffalo come snorting and kicking up the dry dusty earth. They are followed by magnificently painted men, spears in hand, riding their mustangs bareback. They whoop as the ride past pursuing their prey. The women, children and old people of the tribe, who gather their rewards after the hunt, follow them. The Clan Mother follows then to the beat of a slow rhythmic drumbeat. One last clap of the drum and the smoke on the horizon dissipates, then they are gone.

Then, suddenly the train jolts and I am awoken completely from my vision. Theo still sits opposite me, just as he was when I fell asleep. Outside the prairie goes on for endless miles as I stare out of the dusty train window.

Our journey continues, on this last day, as we pass vast great lakes to a waterfall, they call the 'Spirit of the Mist'. Down through Boston and eventually to New York, where our ship to England is ready to be boarded. As we leave the harbour, I turn to look at the newly erected Statue of Liberty, a gift from one republic to another.

I ask her to protect the final part of our journey across the Atlantic. She stands their tall and brave, but a tear, she sheds for the land of the free, and for a forgotten people, that were once native to this new nation.

Across the Rocky Road

From deep within the canyon's belly roars a river wild and
true
A bridge so high suspended, above a gorge.
Where boulders and totems reach for the sky
Far above the misty clouds
Where eagles soar to a piercing cry
As the great bear roams the deep rich forests.

A pine-clad valley freshly burnt in the midday sun.
A cooling breeze from snow laden granite tops
A half dome with cascading waterfall

The sun glimpses through mountain pathways
Where chipmunks scamper and mountain lions roam
An icy pond to chill the black thunderous rain.

A magical kingdom of red dusty canyons beckon.
Carved with mysterious winds over time
Hummingbirds hover, nectar to quench their thirst
Winding paths to archways and pinnacled turrets
Dust storms rage under the blistering dessert canopy
A ghostly place, inhabited now only by Ancestral Native
Spirits.

Across a ridge of Rocky Mountains
Lies fresh untouched spring snow, white and thick.
Whistling smoke puffs from trains of steam
Twisting through endless tunnels and past winding river
bends
Edged with redwood pines, tumbling rocks and mines of
gold.
Memories of pioneers and ghosts of old miners, a nation of
people embedded in the land.

Wild mustangs roam the blue peppered cornflower prairies
Sounds of huffing buffalo grunt as the morning mist arises
Thunder rumbles on distant horizon from blue grey clouds
The heaviness lingers long and painful
Echoes of songs and dances arise across the empty plains
Where once a nation roamed free, now a hidden forgotten
people.

From a Great Lake starts the everlasting journey of the
Mississippi.
As it winds its way deep south to tell of showboats and Madi
Gras,
The heat, the humidity, haunted hospitals where soldiers
once lay to die,
Resonating battle cries of States torn apart.
Magnificent mansions Southern in their day, now covered in
Spanish moss,
As sizzling rain hits the ground, steaming in the hot southern
summer.

To the Queen of the mist, a waterfall pure and true
A spiritual, cascading glacier, powerful and majestic.
A tea party beckons potent and strong, but one that left a
bittersweet taste.
A land of hope and glory!
Finally, a lady standing bright her light guiding the way
Over the land of the free!
A gift from one nation to another, a beacon to guide the lost.
For the Sons of Liberty!
Our last destination, time for our journey to end
Across this wild and inhospitable land
For everlasting memories
"You all come back now!"

Chapter Ten, Part Two:
Rainbow Boy

Summer was here at last, six weeks off from school. Seren remembered last year's summer holiday, camping, in Cornwall.

"Dad, can we put the tepee up today, in the garden?" Seren asked. "It's such a beautiful day."

"OK," replied Dad. "I'll have to dig it out from the under stairs cupboard, it's been there since last summer."

"Why don't we have a BBQ, when Mum comes home from work. Then we can even have a sleep out under the stars," said Seren.

"Let's see what the weather's doing later on. Good idea though. OK let's get the tepee out, and put it up," said Dad.

There was little breeze, as the bees were busy collecting nectar from the heavily narcotic scented honeysuckle. A perfect summer's day in the 'never never'.

The tepee was up, the day was getting hotter, it was going to be a scorcher. Dad made a drink and they both sat in the back garden outside the tepee. Seren went back into the house to find Bess' journal. By the time she had returned Dad had fallen asleep, in the shade under, the apple tree. Seren turned the pages to where Bess and Theo had travelled across North America, on their return journey to England.

Seren started reading about their train journey that took them through the mid-west from San Francisco to New York on the Transcontinental Train.

In the distance Seren could hear a horse neighing. The noise got louder and louder, until she turned around and just beyond the fence was a magnificent looking appaloosa. He cheekily brushed his mane against the fence. Riding the horse was a young Indian boy, much like the one in Bess' journal. His skin was the colour of red umber, striking against his dark hair and black eyes. He wore a skin around his waist, held up by a beaded waistband. A single eagle feather was woven into his hair. Seed beads around his wrist and ankle twinkled in the sunlight.

However, what was most striking, was the rainbow-coloured stone, attached to a leather strap sitting around his neck.

"Would you like to go for a ride?" asked the boy.

"Sure," replied Seren.

She got up and went through the gate. The boy held out his strong hand that Seren took hold of, he pulled her up onto the horse behind him. The boy clicked his heels tugging at the horse's mane (he had no reigns and only a striped woollen blanket on the horses back) the horse turned swiftly into a gallop.

There were open green fields in front of them the sun beating down on their backs. The horse galloped faster and faster, the hot wind blowing through their hair. The scenery, started changing around them, the green leaved trees and grass faded into the dusty dry plains of the great mid-west. The sun was even hotter now and the dry wind was blowing red dust up behind them. The horse began slowing to a trot and then came to a standstill at a watering hole.

Seren and the boy got down from the horse to allow him to drink. They both sat down in the shade and the boy gave Seren a sweet drink,

"What is your name?" asked the boy.

"My name is Seren, which means Star," she replied. "What's your name."

He replied, "Rainbow Boy." Then he started telling Seren the story of how he got his name.

"I am the boy who brought all the colours together. When I was born my mother looked into my eyes and was dazzled to see they were made of different colours. The Medicine Man said I was a special child and one day I would help solve many conflicts and bring hope to our people.

I had a vision in my dream one night, I told my mother who told the Medicine Man, who said I should paint it on my tepee.

A pure white aura surrounds me. Its warms and protects me. I am born into a world of wonder and amazement. The pale glow of ochre mingles with the white. As it becomes stronger and stronger, I bask in its golden shimmer, until it fills the sky with all its radiant magnificence. The burnt orange sun sets across the distant vista. The deep red blood drips from the bleeding sienna sun as it dips below the horizon. The heat of the day gives way to the mellowing greens and browns of autumn's canopy. The frosty icy blue of the wild crashing seas sends a chill down my spine. Light fluffy slate clouds build from the east. Sliver lightning strikes at my heart. I am the ferocity of mighty bruised grey purple storm clouds.

The colours in my vision were afraid so I told them to hold together and the storm would pass and they would be safe and bring hope to the people of my village. They agreed and formed a bow that spread across the sky, as the storm eased and passed. I woke.

As I painted the vision I felt;

I am the scorched blood red earth
I am the glowing orange umber sunset
I am the laughter of the yellow sunflower in the summer meadows
I am the emerald of the forest and the hope of new spring buds
I am the peaceful blue cornflower that grows on the prairies
I am the silence of the deep indigo waters
I am the mystery of the purple dewdrops glistening on a spider's web."

Seren said, "Your story is amazing. Please tell me another one, this time about your people."

As they sat in the afternoon sun a cooling breeze rustled across the dry prairie grassland.

"I will tell you a story," he said, "about my people, but you must give me the first line."

The Story of Colestah

"OK," said Seren. "Long ago there lived a medicine woman, she lived amongst the Wolf Clan of the Sioux, on the high plains. She was well known for her medicine and people would come long distances to see her."

The boy thought for a while then started.

"Her name was Colestah. She was not a native of the Wolf Clan, as all thought. However, she had belonged to the Owl Clan and had been rescued as a young girl. She had very strange markings on her and so the people respected her as she was different. They did not know what to do with her so after a meeting they decided to give her to the Medicine Man of the village to train.

Over time, she learnt many things but the man knew she had a special gift, a power he did not have. She could predict the future; she would have visions that would come true. Her markings would change each time this happened, she would have no memory of the event apart from the new marking that appeared on her body.

She could predict if winter would be long and hard, if summer would come early and when the buffalo would arrive. Her new clan benefited from this. But at times her prediction would be sad, she knew when illness would come and death would visit. But she would also know when their enemies would raid their village.

One day while she was out walking gathering herbs (alfalfa, valerim root and wild rose) to make some medicine, the Great Spirit spoke to her. As he did, she went into a trance.

"Listen, my child, there is a time coming when a people who number as many stars in the sky will come to this land and take it from you and you people. You must warn all you see to preserve their way of life and heritage. But no matter what, the outcome will be the same."

As she came out of her trance, she remembered what had been said and a new drawing had appeared on her body of the Great Spirit talking to her. Then the future was drawn upon her. She hurried back to the village and to the chief to tell him what had happened.

The elders sat round in council passing the talking stick* to each member and they pondered on what they had been told. The elders said she must visit all the other tribes to let them know. She was able to change herself into an owl so she could travel and tell all. Unfortunately, the other tribes did not believe her. And so, she returned home.

Only her own clan believed her. The chief said, "We must leave this place before it is too late."

As predicted a people came from the sea on large boats. It took many years but they tore the locals from the land and their way of life. Only the Wolf clan survived; as the Great Spirit put a protection spell on them, for they had done all he had asked of them. They live in an enchanted world and only from time to time may you get a ghostly impression of them as they move from their summer home on the Great Plains to their winter hunting grounds. If you listen carefully, you may also hear their songs and chants being carried by the wind. This is the end of my story," said the boy.

Once finished his stories, Rainbow Boy said that he would take Seren back home. They climbed back onto Kachina (his name means Sacred Dancer Spirit) and rode back the way they had come. The green grass of Devon returned and the familiar surroundings of home. Seren got down from the horse and thanked him for the ride by giving him a big hug. Rainbow boy said he would come back again and tell Seren another story.

Seren said thank you and waved goodbye as the boy and the horse turned and galloped off into the setting sun. Seren sat back at the entrance of the tepee and thought about her day as her dad started stirring and woke up.

"Right," he said, "it's time to light the BBQ, as Mum will be home soon."

* People would pass the stick around if they had a story to tell, or something important to report.

DEVON

Chapter Eleven, Part One:
Home – Devon, 1889

Once, back in Devon, we settled in a place called Whiteforde, near the village where I was born. The parish is prosperous and on the main coaching road from Plymouth to London. On the outskirts of the parish is a large coaching house, a welcome break for the horses after the steep hill they have to ascend into Whiteford. Down the road is a blacksmith, a post office, a school and bakery. Up on the hill is the white towered church and opposite that is Whiteford House where Sir Buckland lives. There are two farms in the area, on one ridge a dairy farm and the other kept sheep. Exeter nearby is a busy market town with a flourishing quayside.

This was a good opportunity for me to grow my lavender again and make products to sell in the markets. I have also secured a position at the school teaching. There are many children in the parish, but they also come from the surrounding area and the farms. It is an honour to teach the children about the wonders of the world and of the music, art and dance from the different cultures I have lived in. I am writing stories and poems down to read to the children at the school, traditional stories of pixies and witches that once lived on Dartmoor.

Theo spends his time establishing the gardens and greenhouses with plants and seeds that he had collected and stored from all the places they had been too. Finally, his own mini–Kew Gardens.

Charles is now 19 and has gone away to study botany at the newly opened University of Bristol. Florence who is 16 and has just finished school has a job at the big house, but also helps out at the local stables, she loves riding. Sometimes I get to ride as well, in my spare time. My youngest Olivia is 10 and at the village school.

Lately, I have spent time fondly remembering my childhood and the time I spent on the moors with my aunt and cousins at Widecombe in the Moor and my many visits to Haytor and Dartmeet. A letter has come from Ma, who has decided to return home to Devon, it will be such a treat to have her home with me, after so many years. She says the family are all very well and will be fine without her. Now, I wonder through Theo's scented gardens at dusk and I am joined by the night-time faeries. As I sit at the top garden overlooking the view, I reminisce about my travels and happy life with Theo. The night faeries buzz around me until I fall asleep and help me to dream of adventures still to come.

Home

Spiralling in on an African breeze, the swallows bring summer to the green hills and moors of Devon.

The soft yellow primroses now gone are replaced by bright giant sunflowers.

Honeybees buzz around the pond collecting nectar from wild geraniums, while pond skaters dance to their merry tune.

The glasshouse bursting with plants, swelter in the crushing heat as tropical plants mingle with red juicy tomatoes and succulent cucumbers.

A rusty roller sighs as it leans against the red brick wall after a life dedicated to precision.

The croak of the frog and chirp of the grasshopper linger in the afternoon heat.

The hover of the dragonflies darting back and forth drown out the frogs.

Evening comes and the last of the honeysuckle oozes her scent a dangerous and sweet enticing aroma.

The hanging buddleia attracts the painted ladies to their final destination.

The stillness calms the intense heat of the day with every cooling breeze.

Far beyond the golden sands where tourists bathe, lemon and violet hues hang in the sky as the distant rays of sun set behind Devon's piers.

The train hurtles past, hugging the estuary of the Avocet coastline taking the tourists home to lodge. Memories of old as smoke rises from steam trains aboard the Riviera line to hidden coves of Torquay.

For the more adventurous the great tors watch over an ancient seabed of granite, but hark, they do little to give up their secrets of tales of beasts and witches abound.

Glossy blackberries abound, ripening to juicy delight and reflect the sun's rays.

Mist hanging low in the valleys and winding gorge of the river Teign, whilst bluebells lap the reservoirs edge, where foxes come and play.

The soft mossy pathways twist and wind around Fernworthy, a home to trolls and pixies alike, a time to tell stories and enter a kingdom of make believe.

Green woodpeckers forage for food as the buzzards rise above, circling, searching for glimpses of the white stag.

Autumn comes crisp and warming, the leaves turn from golden green to burnished coppery reds, as the first frosts singe their edges.

The swallows leave to warmer African climes, to be replaced by the robin's red breast and his song of winter, as he leaves his footprints in the snow-covered lawns.

Deep snow falls to the howling winds and bending of creaking trees. Everything sleeps now, under a crisp white blanket, buds forming ready for spring.

Silence abounds, winter is here and the pond freezes. Under the dormant icy layer, the encased newts and frogs lie in wait for warmer times.

At last.

Hardy snowdrops are first to bloom, braving the icy cold. The cheeky vibrant crocuses, are next to show themselves. Soft wild daffodils caress the March winds while the exotic tulips soak up the April showers.

All is followed by oriental blossoms of camellias, twisting rhododendrons and blankets of bluebells all heralding the return of spring.

A Poem of the Moors

Beyond high hills and streams of wild
Lay a glade, oh fore told
Where pixies, faeries and mystic folk of old
Do frolic and do play.

An ancient clapper bridge you seek
A guide, to a sacred spot
A place to bathe, in an elixir of life
Eternity ascends a promise within.

A willow the wisp and fabled cries,
Far beyond your wildest dreams
Where woodland creatures large and small
Gather at pools own edge
To gaze upon such beauty as of yet unseen.

For time to go as twilight comes
You see such things you dare not name
High above the moon is born
Cloaked with wisps of grey and wing of bat.
As mist descends it's time to flee,
You dare to look at shadows so deep,
But look, you must for fear awakes,
What hallows can but before you see.

A snap a cry of grim despair,
A glimpse of twinkling stars,
Brings hope of pathways yet unseen,
To which may lead to lands beyond,
This poisoned night time glare.

But to no avail a ripped and tortured shape from beyond the
grave.
A wicker man cursed of witch and twisted limbs he be,
A deathly voice to beckon you in,
Pulled beneath to blood of worms and belly of toads,
Cracked and torn a last silent gasp of life you give.

As Mother Moon looks down with tears of silvery light,
Her spell abounds your eternal life awakes,
With beams of stars, you're drawn upon her, your beauty is
reborn,
To glow above this glade below for all perpetuity.

Chapter Eleven, Part Two:
Pixie Valley

The family had gone for a picnic on the moors, with a cousin who was visiting from New Zealand. A day out to show her the highlights of the area. After the picnic, it was time to walk to Haytor. Once at the top Seren remembered this was one of Bess' favourite spots. She knew that Bess had many adventures playing with her cousins on the moors. Seren remembered a poem that Bess had written in her diary about the pixies and witches that lived in the area.

After they walked around the tor, Seren started seeing faces of animals in the rocks, like monkeys and cats she wondered if the spirits of these animals lived within them. There are many traditional stories from the moors of strange happenings around the tors. Seren thought of where the pixies and witches might live. After a busy day, they returned home and discussed their adventure over supper. Then they all went to sleep to dream.

Here is the dream Seren had.

The fog slowly began to clear, as it still hung to the face of the tor. It left a bright early frosty autumn morn. In the distance Seren could see an old craggy building that looked like a folly. As she got closer, it turned out to be a witch's cottage. It belonged to Haggerty Bag the old witch of the moor. She was well known to the locals as a good white witch who helped strangers when they got into trouble on the moors. Her cottage, surrounded by bracken and fern, lay in a dell on the edge of a valley; the warming hazy sun flickered through the trees. Looking around Seren could see beehives to one side, the bees just beginning to wake up while chickens ran freely, scratching in the dust. The cottage was thatched, and worn in places, with birds flying in and out, catching the early worm. Smoke began curling upwards from the lone chimney stack. Seren knocked the door and Haggerty came promptly, chatting away to herself as she opened it.

"Hello dearie are you lost?" she asked.

"A little," Seren replied.

"Come in and have some tea and breakfast." The smell of sausages drifted from the open fire across the room, enticing her in, Seren's tummy rumbled.

A big fat long haired tortoiseshell cat, called Willow, sat by the fire purring, he stretched and yawned as he looked at Seren. She thought he gave her a big smile as he turned over to go back to sleep. The breakfast was nearly ready. Seren sat at the kitchen table her mouth-watering, Haggerty looked like a good cook.

As Haggerty brought the food to the table Seren heard a clatter of noise from upstairs. "Don't worry," said Haggerty, "it's only Alfie." Seren wondered who Alfie could be as she tucked into the enormous breakfast.

Now Haggerty was a sort of disorganised witch, but one who was always kind at heart and willing to help. Her twisting salt and pepper hair was tinged with the odd shade of purple or red depending on what spell had gone wrong that day, and singed her hair, which was often full of brambles, nettles, or even the odd blackberry. She loved animals and kept all sorts from guinea pigs to bees. She would also have wild animals, nursing hares, rabbits or even foxes, while birds would visit in the spring, during nesting time. Many a day she would sit crocheting or flower arranging or trying out a new spell, which quite often would go wrong, and before she knew it the day had gone and nothing more than a cloud of dust had been achieved.

Today she was in a flap as she was busy preparing for the arrival of her sister Blodwyn.

"My sister the witch of flowers is coming from the Celtic land today, to bless the flowers as they bloom. Now eat up," said Haggerty.

Then Alfie appeared, chattering and squeaking.

"What's the matter?" said Haggerty to Alfie. He chattered away to Haggerty and she seemed to understand every sound he made. Seren was surprised. Why? Because Alfie was a little monkey.

He turned to Seren and squeaked something that sounded like, "Good Morning, how are you and welcome."

"Thank you," said Seren. Who continued eating her breakfast and listening to the conversation between Alfie and Haggerty.

"He's a bit upset with the pixies at the moment. Most of the time they are very helpful, but occasionally they fall out and they play little tricks on each other. Alfie seems to have come off the worst this time, it's all harmless fun."

Seren said she would like to meet the pixies if possible. Alfie squeaked and disappeared back upstairs.

"OK," said Haggerty, "when we have finished washing up, we will go to Pixie Valley, we have time before Blodwyn arrives."

So off they all went, Alfie too. Still a little bit put out, but he seemed an amenable little fellow and was most polite to Seren. What a sight they looked like, a witch, a cat, a monkey and a girl. As they left the dreamy haze of Haggerty's cottage behind them, the bees followed, to where the heather and gorse grew, there the group left them busily buzzing gathering pollen. As the scenery changed so too did the smell. The scent of tannic honeyed blackberries infused with the earthy pungent bracken and mingled with wood smoke drifting on the breeze.

Down a pathway they walked, the banks narrowing all the time leading to a small gorge. Seren could hear water flowing in the distance. The path became wetter and more slippery.

"Be careful, dearie," said Haggerty, "we are nearly there."

As they turned the corner before them, a waterfall, the tallest Seren had seen. The sun dancing through the trees above fanning out rainbows in the spray. The water was refreshing as it hit Seren's lips from bouncing off the stones below.

"This is the Silver Lady Waterfall," Haggerty told Seren. "We need to go behind, hold tight."

They walked behind the secret waterfall to where the pixies lived. Through a tunnel of moss and fern clad walls, silence, it was dark apart from the glow worms, like little white lights lighting the way into the valley beyond. As they emerged, Seren blinked, the pink and violet sky was full of hazy flecks, sparkling dust floating around. Even the rain, as it sprinkled through the sun's rays, was delicate and fresh, looking like gold and silver threads being woven into a tapestry. The pixies lived under mushrooms and toadstools of all descriptions, sizes and colours. Seren had entered a wispy dreamy place where time was still and had no meaning here.

The pixies emerged from their homes, excited about the stranger Haggerty had brought with her. Seren had a wonderful time meeting them and exploring their valley. Alfie was still a bit agitated with the pixies, but Seren was able to pacify him. Two of the pixies came up to Seren and beckoned her to go with them.

"We want to show her something special, is that OK Haggerty?" asked one of the pixies.

"OK, off you go but don't be too long. I have some business to discuss with the head pixie," Haggerty replied.

"My name is Tirana and this is Felipa, come follow us Seren."

"How do you know my name?" Seren asked.

"We are pixies, we know such things. But we must be quick, as what we want to show you only appears at this time of day," they replied.

Seren followed them through some trees into a glade surrounded by ferns, as soft as silk. Drifting in the air were strands of gossamer from a spider's web. In the middle of the glade was a pond, covered with lily pads, where dragonflies hovered. Then the lily pads stared to part, allowing the water beneath to be seen. The water was crystal clear with small particles of coloured glittery sand rising to the surface. The sun's rays filtered into the glade making the colours even more intense.

"Sit back and watch," said Felipa.

The water, the swirled round and round until it rose up into the air, just above the pond, the glittery colours of the sand started mixing together. The water then dropped and left small figures in the air. As they continued moving, they unwrapped their delicate, exquisite translucent wings, dying them on the breeze. Fliting this way and that way, one flew close to Seren. A great big smile on its tiny face, buzz and off it went. Followed by the others.

"This is how faeries are born, here," said Tirana. "See, off they go into the forest to find a new home at the bottom of someone's garden, or round a wishing well."

Seren was spellbound at the magic she had just seen. Seren went back with her new pixie friends to tell Haggerty what she had just seen.

"My, that sounds wonderful, dearie," said Haggerty. "Off we pop then, as it's getting late."

Seren said her goodbyes to the pixies, especially to Tirana and Felipa and thanked them so much for showing her the fairies.

Suddenly on the way back the mist came down early and Haggerty lost her way.

"Oh, cur fuddle," she said, "I am losing my wits, we have taken a wrong turn, and we are near Lilith Birches place, a dark place on the moors. She is a bad witch. I will cast an invisibility spell over you Seren so that Lilith won't be able to see you."

The bad witch was out and about, she did not like Haggerty because she helped people in need. Lilith did not like people as they had let her down in the past and over time; her memories had made her bitter and twisted.

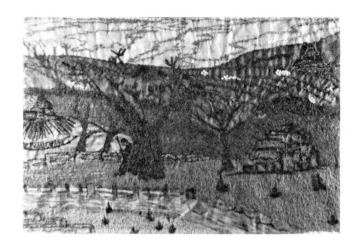

Lilith Birch lived on top of a dark grey granite craggy outcrop near the Devils Cauldron, a dark place of bubbling black water that swirled and swished and went to the deep depths of the earth. Here she would wait for unsuspecting travellers, trap them until they gave her what she wanted, if they did not, she would dispose of them in the cauldron.

Lilith spotted Haggerty Alfie and Willow, she could see that she they were lost and confused. This would be her chance to get rid of Haggerty once and for all.

She tricked Haggerty, Alfie and Willow the cat by pretending to be a person lost and in need of help. Haggerty still confused rushed to help. Lilith then threw off her disguise, Haggerty gasped but she was too slow to react. The bad witch turned the three into stone tors with a flick of her crook.

As Lilith could not see Seren, she managed to escape and found her way back to Haggerty's cottage where Blodwyn was waiting, for her sister.

"Hello," said a sweet magical voice. "Who are you?"

"I'm Seren, a friend of Haggerty. Are you Blodwyn? You must come quick Haggerty, Alfie and Willow have been turned to stone by Lilith Birch."

"That mean old witch, she has always disliked Haggerty, this will be her undoing," said Blodwyn.

Off they went Seren leading the way. When they got there Lilith had vanished and the moon was now shining brightly over the three stone statues.

"Oh my," said Blodwyn, "my poor sister, that Lilith has it coming to her!" she exclaimed. "We must find the Tree of all Knowing she will know what to do to break the spell."

So, they searched the nearby forest. "I know she is here; I can sense her," Haggerty's sister said to Seren. "We must find her while the moon is still full."

Then the next tree they came across yawned and opened up her branches.

"Hello, Blodwyn, my dear," said the tree, "it's been a while since we last met, what are you doing here?"

Seren had never seen a tree like this one. She was dressed in gifts of coins embedded in her bark; ribbons tied to her branches that local folk had left her over many centuries when they prayed to her for help. She was the oldest wisest tree in the forest.

"We need your help," said Blodwyn. "Haggerty and her pets have been changed into stone by Lilith Birch; can your magic break her spell?"

"My magic is not strong enough to break black magic, you must try the three hares that roam this land, they will be able to help you, and tonight they are about. You will see them leaping in the moonlight."

They thanked the Tree of all Knowing, and off they went in search of these three elusive magic creatures. The moon was still young so they had time. From fields to forest to moor they searched asking any passing creature if they had seen the hares tonight. None had, but they all said there was evidence they were about and wished them luck.

Then they looked at the moon and said, "Please shine your light so we can find these hares." Just then, the moon shone the biggest and brightest, it became a silver moon. At that point, they saw three white hares leaping across that moon and they came to land before them.

"We have heard that you have been looking for us, how can we help?" the drove said in unison.

They were ancient magnificent creatures. Blodwyn explained their situation and asked if they could help.

"We have a spell you could try."

"We come to dance in the light of the moon along the river where time is drawn a circle, we form with mist abound grace and elegance a magical glow.

From Avalon a star is formed it falls amongst the dancing core beauty aglow it dazzles and weaves its spell a new dance of daring and romance.

The time is lost; the spell is broke, for a new arc arises the dancers fall and sleep amongst the dewy moss A faded star returns to Evermore To sparkle over dreamtime folk until night-time once more a cloaks."

The hares had fallen asleep, their spell did not work. Blodwyn woke them up.

"We cannot break the spell, it is too powerful, but we know who can, he alone can break the black magic of the moors his name is Old Crockern. We will help you find him. Climb onto our backs and we will leap, hold tight."

So, they did. The vibrant flamboyant moon now glowed a blood orange. After a while they came to the high part of the moor where not many locals went. There was a large tor with very old granite upon it. Just then, they heard a crack in the ground as Old Crockern, stretched and woke up to find the strange party in front of him.

"My, my, what do I have in front of me a strange party, a witch, three hares and a young girl. What can I do for you?" he enquired.

They greeted him back and Blodwyn told him what had happened.

"Lilith has been up to her old tricks again, this time it must stop. First I will need some things to break the spell."

He told them what and off they went to collect them, including some witch's butter*. Seren had to collect a broken piece of crockery with a picture of a cat on it. Blodwyn needed something of Haggerty's, so she returned to the cottage. The hares had the worst task and to retrieve something belonging to Lilith. Fortunately, she was out doing her deeds when they arrived at her hovel. They quickly retrieved what they needed. When they came back, they placed them before Crockern, a broken plate, Haggerty's apron and a picture of Lilith and the witch's butter.

Old Crockern began to cast a spell over them.

"From time and eternity, break stone to flesh, breath life back into heart, cast out demons of old, blessed be the skin and bones arise again and be new."

With that there was a flash of light and Lilith's spell was broken.

When the spell had been broken Haggerty, Alfie and Willow appeared in front of them, the items that were brought had vanished.

"Oh, that was not a nice experience," Haggerty said. "Thank you," she said, and then hugged them all in turn. They danced for joy in the moonlight.

Old Crockern spoke, "Now to deal with Lilith."

The plan was to trick Lilith into an old tapestry that Haggerty had. It hung on the wall in her cottage, so Alfie was sent back to collect it. The rest of them were set the task of capturing Lilith. Crockern disguised them as travellers, lost on one of the moor roads. It was not long before Lilith turned up, never to ignore someone's hardship and turn it to her own advantage. However, she was not expecting them and Blodwyn and Haggerty cast a stillness spell over Lilith. She temporarily could not move so they were able to bind her and remove her crook. By this time, Alfie had returned with the tapestry.

They brought her before Old Crockern, who cast a spell that started to unravel Lilith from her shoes to her clothes to her black dense hair.

"Untie, undo form shoes to hair, thread to thread and back again unravel, unravel no stitch or knot to leave to unweave her magic by crewel to cruel stitch by stitch from hair to shoes a knot at end never to unravel."

At last, Lilith was trapped, never to cast a spell on an expectant traveller again.

Lilith was rewoven into the tapestry. Faintly and ghostly, so that sometimes when one looks at a tapestry, you are not quite sure if there is a figure there or not. To this day Lilith moves from tapestry to tapestry in this way her magic is under control. Next time you see a tapestry have a look to see if she is there.

After that the adventure was over Seren returned to Haggerty's cottage with Blodwyn for a nice cup of blackberry and nettle tea. Haggerty rehung the tapestry on the wall over the fireplace. Seren settled by the fire, falling asleep the last words she heard were that of Haggerty Bag saying, "You must come back and visit again dearie."

Seren woke to find herself safe and sound, back in her own bed. She was hungry for a hearty breakfast after her adventurous and magical dream. She came rushing downstairs eager to tell all of Haggerty, Blodwyn, Lilith and all the creatures she had dreamt of that night. The family hung on her every word enthralled by her tale.

What adventures were to follow?

* Is a common jelly fungus in the Tremellaceae family of the Agaricomycotina. It is most frequently found on dead but attached and on recently fallen branches.

https://en.wikipedia.org

Epilogue

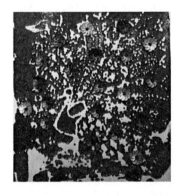

From time-to-time Seren would re visit Bess' diary and the new friends she had made in her dreams. Back in Africa, she had a dream, where she meets Nokwazi, Kagiso and Lesedi and the all had great South African adventures together. Seren would also dream of Mongoose and Sekar and their adventures as they walked home. Occasionally they would be joined by Laxman when Indra could spare him. The three friends were so happy to be reunited. She would dream of shadow puppets, the life and further adventure that Princess Yu-Phin and Prince Anurak would have together. Seren had dreams where Rainbow Boy and Wasiu meet up and became friends and they all would have endless adventures across the North American Plains or somewhere in the South Pacific.

Occasionally the Gods that inhabited the vast area of Oceania would create mischief for the people. Her friends from Australia would also call to her, for help, to fend of strange dreamtime creatures. Seren would always respond when Emu, Koala, Kangaroo and the Magic Man needed her. The elusive Patu Paiarehe would make an appearance and tell Seren stories of their people and Princess Tawera. Finally, closer to home Seren would revisit Haggerty Bag in her cottage. Where Willow and Alfie would greet her, what would ensue were more adventures on Dartmoor that involved magical and mythical beings of the Moors.

So, the dreams, magic and adventure never stopped coming. 'If you dare to dream, dreams really do come true.'

As for Bess, she continued to live her full and adventurous life out in the parish of Whiteford. Where she continued to teach the children at the school, until she retired. She continued to paint and write her stories and poems. She died, peacefully at the age of 97, surrounded by her loving children and their families. Bess' ma had come to live with them from South Africa, she lived another five years where Bess cared for her, when she got ill. Theo died ten years before Bess, while tending his exotic plant collection. They were still very much in love. Florence, her eldest daughter continued to live in the parish and also became a teacher at the school. Charles continued in his father's footsteps and became a successful botanist. While Olivia followed her mother's passion for painting and writing. Bess and Theo had brought their love of the world back to Devon.

They had ventured 'Over the Rainbow'. So why don't you?